MW00709940

# DUTCH

K19 SECURITY SOLUTION

BOOK FIVE

## HEATHER SLADE

DUTCH
© 2019 Heather Slade

All rights reserved. No part of this book may be used or reproduced in any manner whatsoever without written permission, except in the case of brief quotations embodied in critical articles and reviews.

This book is a work of fiction. The names, characters, places and incidents are products of the writer's imagination or have been used fictitiously and are not to be construed as real. Any resemblance to persons, living or dead, actual events, locale or organizations is entirely coincidental.

Paperback:
ISBN-13: 978-1-942200-56-7

# MORE FROM AUTHOR HEATHER SLADE

BUTLER RANCH
*Kade's Worth*
*Brodie*
*Maddox*
*Naughton*
*Mercer*
*Kade*

WICKED WINEMAKERS' BALL
Coming soon:
*Brix*
*Ridge*
*Beau*

K19 SECURITY SOLUTIONS
*Razor*
*Gunner*
*Mistletoe*
*Mantis*
*Dutch*
*Striker*
*Monk*
*Halo*
*Tackle*
*Onyx*

K19 SHADOW OPERATIONS
Coming soon:
*Ranger*
*Diesel*

THE ROYAL AGENTS OF MI6
*The Duke and the Assassin*
*The Lord and the Spy*
*The Commoner and the*
*Correspondent*
*The Rancher and the Lady*

THE INVINCIBLES
*Decked*
*Undercover Agent*
*Edged*
*Grinded*
*Riled*
*Handled*
*Smoked*
*Bucked*
*Irished*
Coming soon:
*Sainted*
*Hammered*

COWBOYS OF CRESTED BUTTE
*Fall for Me*
*Dance with Me*
*Kiss Me Cowboy*
*Stay with Me*
*Win Me Over*

# Table of Contents

# Prologue

Her skin was tan from the sun, and her lips were ruby red. Her shoulder-length inky-black hair was the same color as the thin silk camisole she wore to stave off the heat. When its spaghetti strap slid off her shoulder, I couldn't help but wind it around my finger and pull it just a little lower, causing her to try to shrug away and shoot me a look of confusion.

Up until five o'clock today, I wouldn't have laid a hand on her. Now, all bets were off. I was no longer Special Agent Malin "Starling" Kilbourne's boss. In fact, I no longer worked for the CIA at all, which meant I intended to start fulfilling every fantasy I'd had about the woman who made my blood run hot.

Malin covered my hand with hers. "What are you doing?"

I smiled. "Peeking."

I watched as she looked past me, searching the crowded outdoor patio for the rest of the team that had gone out to celebrate both the end of a mission and my leaving the agency. When her gaze settled on me and she moved her hand away, I took the opportunity to walk her backwards a few short steps until she rested against the cool stone wall of the building.

Her look challenged more than questioned, and when I leaned in to run my tongue along her clavicle, sweet Miss Malin gasped and closed her eyes.

Was she surprised? Had she not seen this coming? Hadn't she felt how the air around us crackled when I got within a foot of her?

I was done denying myself the knowledge of how her naked body would feel under mine. I pulled the camisole a little lower until I could see the tip of her dusty-rose nipple.

*—Malin—*

It wasn't just the heat and humidity of the summer night that made it hard for me to breathe; Thomas "Dutch" Miller, my former boss as of a few short hours ago and star of every fantasy I'd had as a woman, had his hands on me. Not just his hands, his lips and tongue too.

I was used to seeing him in the dark suits he wore to work every day along with a crisp white button-down shirt and a conservative tie. Tonight, he wore a faded blue t-shirt that was the perfect size to show off the muscles I knew he worked hard to maintain and a pair of khaki cargo shorts. His blond hair was cropped close, but I'd heard him say he intended to grow it long now that he was retiring—at least from working directly for the agency. I'd also heard that he planned to join a private firm owned by several former agency operatives.

As much as I wanted to watch as he bent his head and laved the nipple he'd just exposed, my eyes drifted closed. With one hand, I clutched his arm, not to stop him, but in an attempt to hang on for dear life as the man set my already overheated body on fire.

I was disappointed when he drew the strap of my camisole back up to my shoulder, but groaned with equal intensity when he pulled my arm away from my body and studied the tattoo on the soft skin covering my tricep. He leaned forward again and ran the hard tip of his tongue over the right arrow, the one with the shaft piercing a diamond. That one symbolized invincibility. He moved to the left, tracing the feathered arrow that represented liberty, triumph, and independence.

"I like these," he murmured, raising his head so his lips were close enough to mine to touch. "I like them on your skin."

If I could speak, I wouldn't know what to say. The man had equally intimidated and excited me since the day the CIA's human resource officer led me into his office.

"You're mine now, Kilbourne," Dutch had said that day, but not meaning it in the way I'd wanted him to even after a few minutes in his presence.

Part of me had considered asking for a different assignment, but I didn't. Doing so would've been more of a career-killer than lusting after my first boss.

I put both hands under his shirt and rested my palms just above the waist of his shorts. His skin was hot to the touch while mine alternated between scorching and covered in chill bumps depending on where he ran his tongue.

"You're mine now, Malin," he said, his words fulfilling the first fantasy I'd had of what it would be like to be seduced by him. "Let's get out of here."

He took my hand and led me out the back gate of the bar's patio and to his car. He pushed me up against the passenger door and rested his rock-hard body flush with mine.

"Tell me you want this as much as I do," he said, his eyes boring into mine.

"I do," I breathed right before he took my mouth with his in a kiss that was more incendiary than the hottest flame. I knew it would burn; I only hoped I could withstand the pain he'd inevitably cause me.

Everyone knew Dutch Miller was already in love, and it wasn't with me.

# 1

*Dutch*

*Three Years Later*

I studied the woman sitting on the other side of the private plane that would take us from Bagram Airfield back to the States. She'd changed so much since the first day I met her. She was harder, as though someone had rubbed at her skin until it turned into the thick layer she'd need to protect herself both from the bad guys of the world and from men like myself.

She'd said little since I raced in, grabbed her after shooting the man who'd had a gun to her head, and carried her to the waiting transport vehicle.

At first I thought she was in shock, but the only symptoms she exhibited were anxiety and restlessness. She didn't appear either cool and clammy, or to be breathing abnormally. There was no sign of confusion, just out-and-out anger.

"Malin, it's time for us to—"

"Go to hell, Dutch," she spat, refusing to turn her head.

"You could be a little more appreciative, given I saved your ass. You know Orlov was going to kill you."

She folded her arms and looked out the plane's window, so I could only see the back of her head.

"You understand that, right? Your options were to leave your body here on earth while your soul climbed the stairway to heaven, or be here with me. I'd say you went with the better of the two."

"I didn't make the decision, Dutch. You made it for me."

"When would dying be a better option, sweetheart?"

I saw her flinch.

"You can't hate me that much."

Malin shook her head and looked at me. "I was in the middle of a mission. One that I've been working for months." Her eyes bored into mine. "You blew it up."

"Either way, the mission would've ended. The only two possible outcomes after that were you dead or alive."

"Orlov wouldn't have killed me," she said, turning away from me again.

"How can you be so certain? Word we got from the agency was that your in was to act as a trainer for the Islamic State's female recruits. Tell me, Starling, how did Orlov figure into that?"

"Don't call me that, and I just know he wouldn't have killed me," she responded, sidestepping everything else I'd said.

I knew she'd detested the code name since it was given to her by someone above my head at the CIA. I'd never been told who it was.

"All I'm saying is it doesn't add up."

She didn't act like she was listening, so I got up, walked over, and sat in the seat next to her.

"I'm sorry about your op, but I'm not sorry you're safe." I leaned close enough that our arms touched.

She didn't pull away, and there was plenty of room that she could have.

"Malin, baby, look at me."

She shook her head again. "I can't do this again, Dutch. Even if you have no respect for me as an agent, please muster up enough for me as a woman to leave me the hell alone."

There was no reason for me to ask what she meant by respecting her as a woman. I'd done exactly the opposite when I walked away from her all those months ago. More than just walking away—I'd chosen another woman over her.

That same woman would soon be married to my best friend, and there were no two people who belonged together more than they did.

I stood and walked to the front of the plane to use the bathroom when I noticed that Malin had dozed off. Between whatever her real dealings were with the Islamic State, not to mention United Russia by way of Sergei Orlov, the woman probably hadn't gotten much rest in the last several weeks.

"Got a minute?" Onyx asked from the front.

"If we're headed home, I've got a few hours."

Onyx nodded at the copilot, a man I didn't recognize, and stood, motioning toward the galley. He walked out and closed the cockpit door behind him.

"Who is that guy?" I asked.

"Contractor. Listen, I got word from Doc."

"And?"

"What do you think about Indian Springs Island?"

I scrubbed my face with my hand and shook my head. "I don't like it." My orders were to take Special Agent Kilbourne somewhere secure and get to the bottom of what in the hell she'd been doing in Bagram mixed up with the likes of the leader of the Islamic State, Abdul Ghafor, as well as a Russian assassin.

"Why not?"

"I want somewhere more remote."

"It belongs to Gunner. You won't find anywhere more secure."

I knew Onyx was right. Gunner Godet, one of four senior partners at K19 Security Solutions where I was a junior partner, would make sure his island was secured tighter than the CIA headquarters.

"Gunner's got some experience with United Russia," Onyx added.

"We don't know she was after UR."

"Why was Orlov there if the beautiful Miss Malin wasn't after them?"

Inexplicably irritated with Onyx for calling Malin beautiful, I changed the subject. "Brief me on how this will go after we land."

"The plan was to chopper out of Reagan."

"Roger that," I said, distracted when I thought I heard Malin groan.

"Sleeping Beauty must be coming to. I gotta get back to flying the plane."

First beautiful, now Sleeping Beauty; Onyx's words didn't sit right with me, not that I could say why, other than my feelings toward her were proprietary.

I'd saved her life. Wasn't there some legend or voodoo thing that said I was supposed to protect her forever now?

I returned to sit next to her, reclined my seat, and pulled her close enough that her head rested on my chest. She was so damn exhausted, she didn't wake up.

"Sweet girl." I ran my fingers through her hair.

I rested my head against hers, wondering again what in the hell I'd been thinking the night when Alegria called and I ran straight to her. Malin deserved so much more, then and now.

Before she fell asleep, she asked me to respect her as a woman and leave her alone. I did respect her—as a woman, a CIA agent, and as one of the finest human beings I'd ever known. Why did I need to leave her alone to prove that to her?

I was kidding myself if I thought groveling would make her accept my apologies and give me another chance, but if she'd let me hold her, even if only while she slept, I'd take it. Having her in my arms again felt so damn good.

Right now, though, I had to find out what the mission that took her to Pakistan by way of Germany really was, along with how Sergei Orlov had been involved.

My every instinct was screaming at me to protect her from the same government agency on whose behalf she undertook the mission to begin with.

Malin, still soundly asleep, shifted her body and put her arm around my waist. I'd forgotten how easily our bodies molded together, even though I didn't appreciate it at the time. Then, I'd believed a different woman would fit me better than anyone else. As it turned out, we hadn't fit at all.

I closed my eyes, part of me wishing I could turn back time and undo what I'd done that night. Another part of me knew that if things hadn't gone the way they had, I might have spent the rest of my life pining for a woman who turned out to be all wrong for me.

# 2

*Malin*

Hovering in the zone between awake and asleep, I struggled the way I always did. Should I keep my eyes closed, hoping the dream I was having about Dutch would continue, or should I wake all the way up, hoping that the pain of it only being a dream wouldn't linger too long?

I ran my hand over his chest that felt all too real and opened my eyes.

"Hi," he said when I looked up at him.

I tried to move away, but he held me close.

"Go back to sleep. It's a long flight, and I bet you haven't slept well in weeks, if not months."

"Dutch, I…"

"Go to sleep, baby," he repeated, kissing my forehead.

I closed my eyes. Why not let myself rest in his arms for a few more hours? Would it really hurt anything? All too soon, I'd be forced to face the reality of the shitstorm my life had become and accept that, once we landed in the States, it might be months before I saw Dutch Miller again.

My eyes were closed but I couldn't sleep. Even now, after three years of hating him, my body still responded to his as if we'd had sex just last night.

We didn't even need to touch. If Dutch merely looked at me, I'd melt into a pool of whomever the man wanted me to be in that moment—agent, friend, lover—whatever he wanted, whatever he needed, whomever he needed, I'd always been powerless to do anything but give it to him.

How many times had I replayed the events of the night I let him go when he needed someone other than me? *Hundreds.*

I could see it unfold as clearly as if it had happened yesterday. There I was in his kitchen, wearing nothing but a white button-down dress shirt like the ones he used to wear to work and a pair of pink panties, when his phone rang. I should've known by the look on his face, who was calling.

He didn't bother to look up at me before answering. I watched as he paced the length of the kitchen, finally telling the woman on the other end of the call that he'd "be right there."

"She's drunk," he'd said. "At the very least, I have to get her home."

"Go," I told him. "She needs you."

When I came out of the bedroom a few minutes later, he was already gone.

Months went by before I saw Dutch again, and then he'd had amnesia and had no idea who I was. I'd been working the same op then that he'd blown to bits a few short hours ago.

I'd almost blown it up myself that night when the man who stood between me and the organization I was assigned to infiltrate demanded I hand Dutch over to the al-Qaeda bastards responsible for beating him nearly to death before I found him wandering the streets of a small town in Germany.

In that moment, I'd asked myself what Dutch would do. Without having to think about it, I knew he would've done anything to keep the op going. And then he would've turned around and gotten me rescued, just like I had him.

"Tell me about the mission," I heard him murmur.

I sat up and pulled away from him, repeating the lines by rote. "My mission was to infiltrate the Islamic State by acting as a trainer for their female recruits."

He smirked and leaned closer. "You can tell me the truth, baby. I have the necessary security clearance."

What the fuck was he doing? Did Dutch think for one minute that he could seduce me into divulging the true nature of my mission?

How stupid could I be? That was why he'd held me in his arms: to break down my resolve and get me to tell him about my mission. No fucking way in the world was I going to fall for it. Instead, I'd keep the wall I'd built around my heart firmly in place, never letting him penetrate it again.

# 3

*Dutch*

*Why no go on Indian Springs?* said the text I received from Doc when we landed at Reagan International Airport in Washington, DC.

Instead of responding with my own text, I called him. "As I told Onyx, I'd prefer somewhere more remote."

"I'd rather keep you both in the States if possible."

"What about Cokabow Island?" I asked.

"That works. You're sure you don't want any kind of backup?"

"One hundred percent." I couldn't explain why I felt like I had to handle this myself, with as few people as possible knowing where Malin was. It was all about me listening to my instincts. Everyone in our line of work did. We had to. It's what kept us alive.

"There'll be a brief waiting that outlines what little we've been able to find out when you're able to access email," Doc said before ending the call.

I returned to the seat next to Malin's. A few minutes later, Onyx opened the door of the aircraft.

"Ready?"

"Where are we going?" she asked when we got to the tarmac, and instead of heading into the main terminal, I followed Onyx in the opposite direction.

"Heliport."

She didn't question why, but I didn't expect her to; it was common for the agency to provide helicopter transport from Reagan to headquarters.

I was tempted to look at my email and review the brief Doc had sent over while we waited, but decided not to until I had a few minutes of assured privacy. I couldn't risk Malin seeing any of it.

"Hungry?" I asked, turning toward her and touching her neck with the tip of my finger.

She flinched and moved away from me. "I can wait."

"When's the last time you ate?"

"I'm not hungry."

"Not the question."

"Yes, it was. You asked if I was hungry."

"And then I asked when you last ate."

"Let it go, Dutch. I'm exhausted, and I just want to go home."

I nodded, wondering how she'd react once we got in the air and she realized she wasn't going anywhere near home.

17

The helicopter ride would take us as far as Langley. There, we'd catch a transport to Shaw Air Force Base, and then another helicopter would transport us to Charleston, where we'd take a boat over to Cokabow Island, our final destination. It would take us a total of seven hours to get to the private island that belonged to K19 Security Solutions.

"Be right back," I said, not that she was paying attention. Malin Kilbourne had a hell of a lot on her mind, and soon, I intended to convince her to tell me exactly what.

"Where'd the other guy go?" I asked Onyx.

"Don't need him from here on out."

"Who's flying with you?"

"Corazón."

"Never heard of him."

"Her."

"What did you say?"

"Corazón is a woman."

"Oh. Got it." My stomach rumbled; I was fucking starving. "Do we have time to get something to eat?"

"She's bringing food with her."

"Who is?"

"Corazón, dude. Pay attention."

That was the problem; I was so hungry, I couldn't think.

"Don't worry, bro," said Onyx, smiling and grabbing my shoulder. "She's bringing enough for everyone."

"When will she be here?" I checked the time. If we didn't get in the air soon, we'd be arriving in South Carolina at dawn.

Onyx leaned in closer. "She's meeting us at Langley."

"What are we waiting for, then?"

"You see anything out there?"

"Planes. The sky. The tarmac. What's your point, *bro*?" I wasn't sure if it was just because I was hangry, but Onyx was working my last nerve.

"You see a helicopter? Cuz I don't."

I flipped him off and walked back over to Malin.

"Do you need to check in? Who's your handler? Sumner Copeland?"

She shook her head. "I'll check in when I get home."

"You're sure? He's likely trying to make contact."

"Stop pushing me, Dutch. My communication with my handler is none of your business."

She was lying, but now wasn't the time for me to confront her about it. First I had to get her alone and then to tell me the truth about everything, including why she seemed completely unconcerned about checking in with her handler.

"What's going on?"

"What do you mean?" I asked.

"Why are you still here?"

"Transport, baby."

"Bullshit. Tell me what the fuck is really going on."

"You're going off the grid."

"The hell I am."

"You don't have to if you wanna cut to the chase and tell me what your mission was really all about."

"You're letting the spy biz go to your head."

I smiled. "Yeah?" Damn, I liked this woman. How had I forgotten how much?

"Who authorized me going off the grid?"

"I haven't read the brief yet."

"There's a brief? Let me read it."

"No can do, baby."

*"It's about me. Let me read it, goddammit."*

"Keep your voice down." I grabbed her arm and led her outside.

Malin's eyes were wide, and I could feel her heart rate pick up beneath my fingers that rested on her pulse. "Am I being burned?"

"Not that you're jumping to conclusions or anything."

"This is my life, Dutch. Don't fuck around with me."

"What happened to you?"

She glared at me and put a hand on her hip. "What do you mean?"

"I don't remember such colorful language."

"Fuck off, Dutch. That colorful enough for you?"

"I didn't say I wanted to hear more of it. Although, in a way, it is kinda sexy."

Her knuckles were white, and she was digging her nails into her own palms while shooting daggers at me through her hazel eyes. Now probably wouldn't be the best time for me to tell her how much I loved those eyes.

"Why would you think you were being burned, Malin? Because I blew up your op? I'll tell you what, the agency insisted we didn't. It was a condition of them giving us Ghafor's twenty."

"And yet you did it anyway."

"Yeah, I did. We already talked about why." I looked outside when I saw the helicopter approaching. "Time to go."

"Dutch?" She put her hand on my arm. "Am I being burned? Just tell me the truth."

She spoke softly, so I did the same, leaning closer. "I haven't heard anything to indicate you were. You're going off the grid for your own protection. I'll tell you this much. You're headed to Langley and, from there, to Shaw."

"I'm asking you again: who authorized this?"

"I did." She probably thought I was being a smart-ass, but I'd just told her the God's honest truth.

Malin bit her bottom lip and followed me out to the helicopter.

Once she was in her seat, I climbed in next to her. Whoever the woman was who was bringing food to Langley better bring a hell of a lot of it. If not, I'd swipe a car and go get a few bags of burgers.

"What's wrong?" she asked.

"I'm starving."

Malin nodded.

"I could really go for some of your spaghetti and meatballs right about now."

She scowled at me and turned her head.

"What?"

"Nothing."

"Come on, I told you where we're going."

Her head spun back around. *"What did you say?"*

"I said I told you where you're going."

"That isn't what you said. You said 'we're.'"

"Same difference."

Malin unfastened her safety harness just as Onyx finished his preflight check.

"Who's unbuckled?" he shouted.

I reached over, refastened her harness, and then gave Onyx a thumbs-up.

Malin didn't look at me for the rest of the quick flight. Soon we'd be touching down at Langley, and then I'd likely get an earful.

# 4

*Malin*

I was as angry as I was terrified. I had to figure out a way to get Dutch to be straight with me about how much the CIA knew about my whereabouts.

If they were the ones who had authorized him to escort me back to the States, and had further approved my "disappearance," then I needed to get the hell away from him before he or anyone else figured out what had really been going on in Islamabad.

It wasn't the agency who had issued the edict about not blowing my op; I had. All it took was intercepting a message from Striker to my handler, Sumner Copeland, and then continuing the conversation as if I were him.

Dutch and the K19 team also believed it was the agency who had given them Ghafor's location. Again, they hadn't; I had.

Somehow, I had to find out whether the CIA knew I'd abandoned my original mission almost as soon as I arrived in Germany or that I was no longer in Pakistan.

As it was, I had no idea whom I could trust, starting with my handler, his boss, Kellen McTiernan, all the way through the layers of supervisors and deputies that ultimately answered to James Flatley, the current Director of the Central Intelligence Agency.

"I need to know who you're working for, Dutch," I said as we walked from the helicopter into the terminal building.

"I already told you."

"You said you authorized me going off the grid."

Before he opened the door for us to go inside, Dutch pulled me closer to him.

"If you haven't had the means or the inclination to tell them, then the agency has no idea where you are or even that you're no longer in Pakistan. K19 isn't talking, and we left no witnesses. Do you understand what I'm saying?"

I nodded, praying he was telling me the truth.

If he was waiting for a tirade, he wouldn't get it. Two could play his game. I had no intention of giving up more than I already had.

Onyx walked past the waiting area where they sat in silence and then backed up. "Food's here."

Dutch looked ready to run in Onyx's direction, but waited for me to stand up.

"Go."

"Not without you."

"I can't run. Where would I go, Dutch?"

"I won't eat until you do."

"That's stupid. I told you before I wasn't hungry."

"When did you last eat?"

When I shrugged, Dutch walked over and held his hand out to me. "Come on, baby. Let's go eat."

"Don't," I snapped.

"Malin, you need to eat."

"And you need to stop with this 'baby' bullshit."

Dutch smiled. "I will if you eat."

I studied him. "Fine," I muttered, walking past him. He put his hand on the small of my back as we walked down the hallway in the direction of something that smelled absolutely delicious.

We entered what looked like a crew break room and saw a feast laid out on one of the long tables.

"What's all this?" Dutch asked, walking over to a woman. "Dutch Miller," he said, holding his hand out.

"Sofia Descanso. Pleasure to meet you, sir," she responded, shaking his hand.

I looked at the woman neither man had introduced me to. "I'm Malin," I said.

"Nice to meet you, ma'am."

"Should I call you Sofia?"

"That works."

"What's your background?" I asked, taking a second bite of the best paella I'd ever tasted.

"Flew an F-15C Eagle until I separated from the Air Force a few months ago."

"Why did you leave active duty?"

"A lot of reasons, but mainly because the stress of how low our pilot numbers were was getting to be too much for me to handle."

"How bad is it?"

"It isn't a secret that the Air Force is close to twenty-five percent short of how many we should have in the air."

I'd heard they were struggling, but I hadn't realized the extent. "Why do you think that is?"

"Again, a lot of reasons. Vicious cycle of them extending pilots' deployments, deploying them more frequently, and pulling fighter pilots from other squadrons to augment those going overseas. Plus, standing up squadrons of pilots flying remotely piloted aircraft like the Predator and Reaper took a huge bite out of the fighter pilot community. The number I heard quoted was over two hundred."

"What does that number represent?"

"Ten percent of the ten percent they're down. It doesn't sound like much, but when we're already low eighteen hundred, why would they snatch two hundred more?"

I shook my head. "What did you do in between? Any agency work?"

"I wasn't interested in intelligence work, not that they came calling."

I did my best to control my sigh of relief, looking up at Dutch when he walked in our direction. I almost laughed when I saw the amount of food he'd piled on his plate before sitting down next to me.

"Oh my God," he said after taking the first bite. "Why are you a pilot instead of a chef?"

"I've thought about it."

"You should do a lot more than think."

"Working for K19 helps," said Sofia.

"Yeah, money's a little better than when you're active duty."

Sofia laughed. "A little?" Then she looked at me. "It's another reason I left," she murmured.

"I agree with Dutch. I spent some time in Spain, and this is still the best paella I've ever had."

Sofia beamed at me.

When Onyx's phone buzzed, he looked at the screen first and then at Dutch. "Time for us to go."

"No f'ing way," Dutch said through another mouthful of food. "I am not leaving until I eat at least another five or six plates of this stuff."

"We can bring it with us. That's what my plan was anyway," said Sofia, smiling.

"Yeah? Damn, woman, I think I love you."

# 5

*Dutch*

"Got a minute?" I said to Onyx.

"Sure," he answered, following me into the hallway.

"Fill me in on her background."

He rolled his eyes. "Do you ever read your briefs?"

"Tell me her fucking background."

"Descanso is a pilot who's coming on board as a full-time contractor for K19. She's been fully vetted by Doc, Gunner, and Razor."

Three of the four original K19 partners had approved her employment, so I wouldn't question it further—at least not for now.

"Malin's safety is paramount to me," I mumbled.

"I know it is," said Onyx. "We all do. That's why we're here, bro. Do you know how much money we're burning in fuel alone?"

"You got a problem with K19 funding the safety of—"

"Knock it off, Miller. That's not what I'm saying. I'm in, okay? I mean, *Jesus*. Do you somehow not realize I've been with you since Bagram?"

"Sorry," I said. "I need more food."

"Me too, asshole."

"One more thing, Onyx. Who knows that you and Descanso are involved?"

"Nobody." Onyx looked down at the floor. "Not even her."

I smiled and grabbed the man's shoulder like he'd done to me earlier. "I think you're wrong about that, bro."

Onyx shook his head.

"Did you see the spread of food in there she made for you? If you don't think that means something, you oughta get outta the spy biz."

It was after midnight when we landed at Shaw, which meant that since the only access to the island was by boat, we wouldn't head over until morning.

"We'll stay somewhere in the historic district tonight so we can leave first thing in the morning," I said to Onyx.

"Sounds good."

"Got any ideas where?"

"For you?"

I shook my head. "For all of us."

Onyx looked away. "I made other arrangements."

"Good for you, *bro*." I hated that expression, but between Onyx and me, it worked.

"I've heard good things about the Yellow Jasmine."

"I'll check it out."

"They're great about respecting peoples' privacy."

I raised an eyebrow.

"I don't know from personal experience. I just know celebrities stay there sometimes."

"If they're good about privacy, how do you know about the celebrities who stay there?"

"I read it somewhere."

After looking online, I settled on a different place. The Meeting House Inn was highly rated, right near the water, and one of the most romantic places to stay in all of South Carolina. Only trouble was, they only had one room left.

I found Malin coming out of the ladies' room followed by Sofia.

"We'll stay in town for the night," I said before turning to Sofia. "It was nice to meet you, and thanks for the amazing grub."

"You can take it with you."

"Nah. I appreciate it, but…"

"I can make more. You can't."

"Twisted my arm, then."

"I'll go get it together," Sofia said before walking back toward the break room.

"I take it she's not staying at the same place we are."

"No, but I can't say where she is staying. Onyx was vague about their plans."

"So you think they're together?"

"Don't you?"

Malin grinned. "Oh, yeah."

It was probably stupid on my part, but I decided not to tell Malin about the shared room until we arrived at the inn. Given how late it was, finding another place would be near impossible, and as exhausted as we both were at this point from traveling, I hoped she'd just accept it without making too much of a fuss.

"I'll take care of getting us checked in," I said, motioning for her to take a seat by the fireplace in the inn's main room.

I didn't have a hell of a lot of personal items with me, but Malin didn't have any. Tomorrow, before we left for the island, we'd need to go shopping.

While I waited for the woman to finish checking us in, I sent a text to Onyx. *Need some gear. Are you and the copilot around tomorrow?*

*Already taken care of. The house is well stocked.*

*I meant clothes and shit,* I answered.

*So did I.*

If someone had thought of clothes—and shit—they must've thought of food too, right?

I signed the piece of paper the woman behind the desk set in front of me.

"How many keys would you like?"

I looked over my shoulder to where Malin sat. It didn't appear she was listening, but I held up one finger rather than answering.

"Enjoy your stay, Mr. Peabody," said the woman as I walked away. "You too, Mrs. Peabody." The woman waved at Malin.

"You can't be serious," she said once we were in the elevator. "You only got one room?"

"It was all they had."

"Dutch—"

I held up my hand. "I'll sleep on the couch."

She nodded and folded her arms in front of her.

When the elevator opened on our floor, we walked down the corridor to the room. I put the card in the reader and motioned for Malin to go ahead of me.

"The couch, huh?"

I walked in behind her and saw that there was one bed and a single nightstand in the small room. There was hardly enough space for me to sleep on the floor, not that I'd make that offer.

"We're adults. We can handle sleeping in the same bed for one night."

"Right," she answered, turning her back to me.

I walked over and put my hand on her shoulder. "Hey, look at me."

Malin shook her head.

"Please?"

She turned around slowly.

"I didn't mean that the way it sounded. What I meant was, I'll respect your space, Malin, even though I'm sleeping next to you."

"Gee, thanks." She turned away again.

I pulled my hand back and ran it through my hair. "I'm trying to do the right thing. Hell, I'm trying to say the right thing."

Malin sat on the edge of the bed. "What's really going on, Dutch? Tell me the truth. Why are we here? Who assigned me to you?"

I wanted to ask one of those questions of her. If I knew what was "really going on," what she was mixed up in, I could help protect her a lot better than I could, acting on blind instinct alone.

"I already told you that I was doing this on my own."

"Why?"

I paced the short expanse of the room. "I know you're in over your head."

Her shoulders went up, but before she could respond, I sat on the bed, next to her.

"Just like I was in over my head when you found me in Germany. Just like Mantis was in over his head when he decided to make a deal with Ghafor to exchange his life for mine. Just like Alegria was, trying to do the same thing. And Gunner with Zary, and even Doc with Merrigan. Every op, every mission, there are times we're in over our heads and we need our teammates to help us out."

She didn't say anything.

"Who's your teammate on this, Malin? Who has your back? I'm guessing it's not Sumner Copeland."

She shook her head.

"Who, then?" I waited, but she didn't respond. "You wanna know why I'm here. There's your answer. I'm the one who's got your back. You may not be ready to tell me what you're involved in, but I'm here anyway."

She took a deep breath and turned her head away. I knew two things. First, she had tears in her eyes, and second, she wouldn't want anyone to see them, especially me.

"You're in danger, and I'm taking you somewhere safe, somewhere where you can hit the reset button, debrief, fill the tank, whatever you wanna call it."

"Why?" she asked again.

"I just told you why."

"Who's funding this?"

"What difference does it make?"

"Because whoever is funding it, wants something."

She was right. There were a lot of things "somebody" wanted. I wanted to keep her safe. I also wanted to know what her mission had really been, who was involved, and how she'd gotten in so deep that Sergei Orlov showed up in Islamabad.

Why was K19 funding it? Because I'd asked them to. If they'd turned me down, I would've done it all on my own. Maybe I'd still offer, depending on how long this went on and how deep in trouble she was.

The bottom line was K19 had agreed to pony up the money because they wanted to know what her mission had been too, and they probably wanted in on it. Not for the money, though. It was more about their collective commitment to ridding the world of as many of the bad guys and as much of the evil as they could.

The partners, both junior and senior, were all fortunate enough to earn plenty of money. It made living our everyday lives easier, particularly when the bad guys came knocking on our front doors, necessitating the elaborate security systems we had to have installed in our homes. Or to cover the cost of jet fuel when one of us or someone we cared about needed to be rescued, removed from danger, or taken off the grid.

"What do you want, Dutch?"

"You're gonna hate me if I tell you."

"Tell me anyway."

"I want another chance with you."

"You're doing all this because you want to fuck me again? Right."

I flinched. "There are a lot of reasons why I'm doing this, Malin. One of them is because I know I hurt you, and I sure as hell wish I hadn't."

She stood and stormed over to the door, but I beat her to it. With my back up against it, I didn't stop her when her hand came up to slap my face. I didn't stop her the second time either. The third time, though, I grabbed both of her wrists. "Enough," I whispered, pulling her close as she cried on my chest.

At some point, we both fell asleep on the bed, but for me, it wasn't soundly. Every time Malin moved even a fraction of an inch, I woke up. If she tried to turn in her sleep, I'd tighten my grip, forcing her to stay nestled against me. It was as though by having her there, all the pain I'd caused her could flow from her body into mine. I'd carry all of it for her, forever, because I'd been the one to dump it on her in the first place.

Now, here, I could take it all back, and at the end of our time together in South Carolina, she could choose to leave or stay, but whichever choice she made, I wanted her to do it pain-free.

When I opened my eyes and saw it was light out, I knew I should wake Malin so we could leave for the island before the historic downtown filled with its daily throng of tourists. I couldn't bring myself to do it, though. Who knew how long it might be before she let me hold her in my arms again? It would be longer still before she shared a bed with me again, if ever.

Instead, I breathed in the perfect scent of her. Only now did I realize how much I'd missed it. I ran my fingers over the curve of her neck, down her arm, and then rested my hand on her hip. I resisted the impulse to lean down and touch my lips to hers, knowing if that was how I woke her, she'd probably slap me again.

"Hi," I said when she opened her eyes and looked into mine.

"What time is it?" she asked, attempting to roll away.

"I don't know," I answered, tightening my grip.

I wasn't sure what I'd expected her to do, but it sure as hell wasn't to cup my cheek with her palm.

"Thank you."

"For?" I asked.

"Lots of things."

"Yeah? I'd be open to hearing all of them."

I added the soft, sweet smile she gave me to the list of things I hadn't realized I missed about her.

"Letting me cry, and not saying anything about it."

I nodded.

"Not making a move on me even though we're in bed next to each other."

"That wasn't easy." I tried to make it sound like a joke, but it didn't, and it wasn't.

"For bringing me here."

That wasn't something I would've expected her to appreciate, but I was relieved she did. Would she still thank me when she realized I had no intention of letting her leave once we got to the island? At least not until I knew every last detail about her mission.

"Are you hungry?" she asked.

"Pretty much always."

"I remember that about you."

"Impossible to forget."

"Where's the food Sofia made?"

I hit my forehead with my fist. "I left it in the back of the car."

"Oh."

"How much do you think it would cost if I paid her to make it all again?"

"Would it matter?"

"What? The cost?"

She nodded.

"You're right. I'd pay whatever price she demanded."

"Text Onyx."

"Good thinking, baby."

I felt her tense and wanted to hit myself in the head a second time. I'd promised not to call her that. "Sorry," I muttered. "I know you don't like that."

When she didn't say anything, there were so many other things I wanted to say, but each one would make her tenser than she already was.

"Dutch?"

"Yeah…Malin?" God, I'd almost called her "baby" again.

"I need to use the restroom."

I smiled and loosened my hold. As soon as she left, I missed feeling her body next to mine.

"Would you like to explore Charleston today?" I asked when she came back and sat on the edge of the bed.

"Can we? I mean do we have time?"

"We aren't on any kind of schedule. It's up to you."

"I've never been here before."

I motioned toward the window. "It's a beautiful day to take a walk along the battery, maybe head downtown to the market."

"That sounds really nice."

# 6

*Malin*

It wasn't as though I hadn't cried over Dutch Miller before, but not like I did last night. Not the gut-wrenching sobs I couldn't have stopped no matter how hard I tried—so I hadn't bothered trying at all. Instead, I'd clung to the very man that caused me so much pain to begin with. I let him stroke my hair and hold me close to him.

The only thing I hadn't done, that I would never do, was let him creep back into my heart. No one could live through a second annihilation like the first one he put me through.

Dutch had put his arm behind my knees and carried me over to the bed. After setting me on it, he'd lain down next to me and pulled me toward him so my head rested on his chest.

He hadn't said a word. It was as though he knew that if he did, he'd break the spell that allowed me to let out all the pain, anguish, anxiety, and fear my body had kept pent up inside for the past several months.

With one hand, he'd massaged my scalp while the other rested on the small of my back. That was the way I'd fallen asleep and the way I woke up.

"Good morning, y'all," said the woman who had greeted us the night before. "Are you ready for some shrimp and grits?"

My eyes met Dutch's. I didn't want to be rude, but I really wasn't hungry, and even if I was, shrimp and grits for breakfast didn't appeal at all. Coffee sounded good, though.

"We're going to take a walk and work up an appetite," Dutch answered.

"There's a nice park right across the street called White Point Garden. It's on the edge of the confluence of the Ashley and Cooper rivers. If you look out into the harbor, you'll see Pinckney Castle—it looks like a fort— and then farther out, there's Fort Sumter," she explained. Then she poured us both a to-go cup of coffee from her French press even though neither of us had asked.

"Major General Charles Cotesworth Pinckney owned most of the land on White Point after the end of the Revolutionary War. You'll see his name on streets and buildings throughout the historic downtown." She also handed Dutch a map. "You can catch a carriage ride down by the market too," she told him, opening the map and pointing to the intersection of two streets.

"Thank you, ma'am." He led me outside to the porch. "I guess she gave us our marching orders."

"She's sweet."

"I read on the website that she's one of Pinckney's descendants."

"She's proud of her heritage."

The weather was warm for January as we strolled the streets of Charleston, marveling at the big old mansions, most of which were designated as historic landmarks.

"I had no idea that Charleston dated back to the sixteen hundreds," I said.

When Dutch didn't respond, I turned to see if he'd heard me. He seemed distracted by something on his phone.

"Everything okay?"

"Yes, fine. Just touching base with Onyx."

"Do we need to leave?"

Dutch shook his head. "No, he and Sofia are going to meet us. If that's okay with you."

"I'd like that." I'd enjoyed talking to Sofia.

We kept walking up the main street until we arrived at the City Market. Onyx and Sofia were waiting at the entrance to the blocks-long historic building where merchants gathered daily to sell their wares.

"Good morning. How was the inn?" Sofia asked.

"Fine. Where did you stay?"

"I have a place over in Mount Pleasant. It's across the bay." Sofia pointed to a bridge that spanned the width of the harbor where a cruise ship was docked.

"It's beautiful here."

"It's home for me. My family has lived here for three generations. My great-grandfather used to joke that he was a Spanish pirate, but I think he was stationed here after World War II and liked it so well, he bought some land."

"It's a nice story."

Sofia smiled. "It is. Either way, he's my hero."

"Who's hungry?" asked Dutch.

"He's always hungry," I muttered.

He reached over and put his arm around my shoulders. "Let's take a carriage ride before we have lunch."

"Sure you can wait that long?" I mumbled.

Dutch kissed my temple. "I want you to be able to see Charleston before we leave for the island." When he did it a second time, I looked over to see if Onyx or Sofia were watching. I pulled away when I saw they both were.

*What was I doing?* God, it was so easy to fall into the way things used to be between us, and I couldn't do that. Never again could I fall for Dutch Miller or his… his…fucking sexy-as-shit smile.

We weren't a couple. We hadn't been since the night he left me for Alegria.

"I wish you wouldn't keep shutting me out," he said, pulling me closer to him.

"Don't." When I pushed away from him, there was hurt in his eyes and that was too damn bad.

I hadn't walked out on Dutch. He had on me. If his feelings were hurt, he had no one to blame but himself.

"I brought more paella for you," Sofia said to him.

Dutch rubbed his stomach. "I can't tell you how happy that makes me."

Food could keep him that way because I sure as hell wasn't going to.

# 7

*Dutch*

I'd spent a lot of time in Charleston, but everything seemed new to me, seeing it through Malin's eyes.

The carriage ride the four of us took went from Broad Street, where most of the shops and restaurants were, over near the inn where we'd spent last night. The driver, who was a fifth-generation Charlestonian, talked the whole way, throwing in stories about his family and his opinions about what he felt the historical society did well and what he thought they fell short on, into the scripted tour.

"What are those?" Malin asked, pointing to steel rods that had been drilled from one side of a house to the other. Many of the homes we'd seen along the way had them.

"Most of these homes have been around for over two hundred years, young lady. Which meant they survived the 1886 earthquake. We lost sixty of Charleston's finest residents that year. Not to mention the millions in damage." He pointed to the rods Malin had asked about. "Not that I think those dang fool things would do any good if we had another quake."

"Which one is your favorite?" I asked her when the driver turned down the street where the fanciest of all the homes were located.

"Definitely not that one. It's too big," she answered, pointing at a sign that read Calhoun Mansion.

I had to agree, especially when the driver told us it was the largest privately owned home in all of South Carolina and that one man lived alone in its thirty-thousand square feet.

"I like that one, with the big porches on the side."

The house Malin had pointed at was painted white with black shutters, and the porches were rounded instead of rectangular like most of the others in the historic part of town. I had to admit a welcoming feel that I couldn't have described.

"Those are called piazzas, ma'am. And the family who owned that house, well, they couldn't have children, so every Sunday, they'd go over to the orphanage and bring all the kids to their house for an ice cream social."

"That was nice of them," she mumbled.

"You okay?" I asked when I saw her brush a tear away. I laughed when she slugged me.

When we ended up back at the public market, Sofia led Malin inside.

"How is she doing?" Onyx asked once they were gone.

"Fragile, but a lot of that is my fault."

"You did what you had to do."

"Right." I didn't bother telling Onyx that what he was referring to wasn't what made her fragile.

"What did you find?" I asked when I found Malin watching a woman weave seagrass baskets. "They're so beautiful." She ran her hand over a smaller-sized one.

"What's your name, child?" asked the weaver.

"Malin," she answered, walking over to look at the delicately woven Christmas ornaments.

"You pick out your favorite, Miss Malin, and it'll be my gift to you."

"You don't have to do that."

The woman stood, grabbed her cane, and walked over to the small tree where the ornaments hung.

"Which one, child?" I heard the woman whisper. "If you don't pick, I will."

"I like the angel," Malin answered.

"That's the one I would've chosen for you."

The woman took the ornament off the tree and wrapped it in tissue paper.

It made me want to buy every single basket the woman had for sale just to thank her for being so kind to Malin.

"That angel will watch over you, child. It isn't just for Christmas. You keep it with you always."

By the time we left Charleston to head over to the island where Malin and I would be staying, it was chilly, giving me the perfect excuse to put my arm around her. She didn't seem to mind. In fact, when we hit the wake of a bigger boat and were sprayed with cold water, she almost climbed on my lap.

Twenty minutes later, we'd crossed the waterway and were pulling up to the dock.

"Please tell Sofia we said thanks again," I said to Onyx, who helped me carry the bags of her food up to the main house.

He set the bags on the counter and handed me a piece of paper. "You can order whatever supplies you need from here. You know the drill for the island's security, right?"

I nodded. "I spent a month here after that op in Malawi." There was something about the house I'd fallen in love with the first time I set foot in it. It wasn't fancy and that suited me just fine.

Like many of the residences in Charleston, this one had three levels, with piazzas facing southwest to take advantage of the island's breezes. The main difference between this house and those, was it was built on stilts.

The outside was covered in a mix of yellow pine and cypress clapboard that had been cured in salt water for hardness, making it rot and termite resistant. It was painted in the pastel colors used so often in this part of the south—dark Charleston green, pink, and salmon.

The inside was modestly furnished with casual decor. Big sofas sat in the main living room on the first floor, facing two walls of windows along a third with French doors leading out to a piazza like the ones we saw on our carriage ride. The ones on this house, like most of those on the mansions downtown, were squared off on the corners rather than round.

The original owners had splurged on the kitchen more than anything else with a built-in refrigerator, an eight-burner high-end cooktop, and a double oven that also had a warming drawer. The large island in the middle had a brick base and tile countertops that were painted to look like stone.

There were three bedrooms and two bathrooms on the second level, and the master was by itself on the third. It had its own luxurious bathroom, two walk-in closets, and a large sitting area near the door to its piazza.

"If you need anything else…" said Onyx.

"Roger that. Thanks, bro."

"Oh, and Doc said he'd check in later."

"Roger that too."

Out of the corner of my eye, I saw Malin walk into the kitchen.

"As I told Dutch, if you need anything…" Onyx waved the piece of paper with the supply company info on it at her. She walked over, took it from his hand, and set it on the counter.

"Thank you," she said, hugging him. "And thank Sofia for me too. Not just for the food."

"You got it." Onyx walked toward the door. "I feel like I forgot something, but you know how that is. I'll remember by the time I get to the dock, and I'll send you a text."

"I'll walk down with you," I offered.

"Everything is secure, including communication," Onyx said when we got back to the boat. "Doc had a guy he knows at Shaw come over yesterday and test it all out. It's bulletproof."

I hoped we wouldn't have any reason to find out whether it was or not.

I took my time walking back up the trail to the house, wondering what my next step should be with Malin.

When my phone buzzed and I took it out of my pocket, I saw it was a call from one of the K19 partners.

"Miller," I answered.

"Dutch, it's Doc. Onyx tells me you're on the island."

"That, we are."

"Got everything you need?"

"We do, Doc. Thank you."

"I wanted you to know that there's a small amount of chatter about Orlov."

"From?"

"McTiernan."

Kellen "Money" McTiernan had been promoted to the position formerly held by Striker Ellis who was now a K19 partner. I didn't know a hell of a lot about the man; I'd only worked with him once. He seemed like more of an analyst than an agent. Word was, though, that he had an astronomical IQ and to watch your back around him.

"What have you heard specifically?" I asked.

"That the Russian disappeared in Islamabad."

"Disappeared?"

Doc laughed when I did. "Evidently, the body hasn't turned up yet."

"Was there an agency-known connection between Kilbourne and Orlov?"

"Not that they're willing to admit, Dutch. Although if there wasn't, they wouldn't be starting to chatter."

"And when Orlov's dead body turns up?"

"My guess is that word will go out that they believe Malin was killed too."

"And thus...burned."

"I don't think so."

If I could work with anyone on the face of the earth, I was thankful it was Doc Butler. I loved the way the guy's mind worked. He was smart as all get-out, and when someone was in the trenches, there was no better man to have fighting alongside them.

"They want her," Doc added.

"My thoughts too, but why?"

"I don't know yet, but if you can get her to talk, even a little, I want a full report."

"Roger that."

I disconnected the call, trying to shake off the feeling of foreboding that had settled over me. Just because the CIA was sending out feelers about Orlov, didn't mean they were looking for Malin. Even when they did, I hoped I'd covered our tracks well enough that it would take them a damn long time to find her.

My feeling of foreboding worsened when I got back to the house and couldn't find Malin in it anywhere. Rather than panic, which I was about to do, I went outside to look.

Ten minutes later, I spotted her off in the distance, running the island's trails. While I hadn't yet changed out of the clothes I'd been wearing for two-going-on-three days, she must've found both workout wear and running shoes.

I got that Malin needed to burn off energy. We'd both trained all our lives, staying in the best shape we could. When missions prevented us from getting the exercise our bodies needed, it could be both physically and mentally painful.

My heavy boots made for shitty running shoes, so I went back to the house, hoping Onyx had gotten some for me too.

Twenty minutes later, I'd changed and was back on the crest, looking for Malin. This time I spotted her down on the beach. Instead of running, she was sitting on the sand.

I took the most direct route I could find, which wasn't saying much. The overgrown vegetation on the island was lush with wild olive, red cedar, laurel cherry, and Sabal palm trees beneath which grew beautyberry, yaupon, wax-myrtle, and curlyleaf yucca plants. My favorite, though, was the purple sea lavender that grew alongside the goldenrod and yellow jessamine. While the trees, shrubs, and plants were beautiful, the density of it all made navigating the already rocky terrain that much more difficult.

After what felt like a hundred switchbacks, I walked out onto the beach, holding my side and trying to catch my breath.

"I was just about to head back." Malin stood in front of me, hands on her hips.

"Have mercy," I said between deep breaths.

"How long has it been, Dutch?"

"Shit. I don't know. Feels like a year, but probably more like a month." Truth be told, I had no idea when I last ran as far as I did today. It would've been one thing if the trail had kept going down, but nope, more than half the time, I felt like I was gaining elevation rather than losing it.

While it couldn't be much more than fifty degrees out, I pulled my sweat-drenched shirt over my head, tossed it on the sand, and sat on it.

"Ew." Malin groaned and sat next to me.

"What?"

"That shirt is going to be mighty gritty when you put it back on."

"Whatever," I muttered, lying back on the sand that would now be in my hair too. I really couldn't have cared less when Malin lay down next to me.

"It felt good to run in less than a hundred degrees."

"I hear you, girl." I'd hated every minute I spent in the Middle East, and it had been far too many. If there was ever anything that might make me consider retiring, it would be being assigned another mission in a place like Syria, Somalia, Iraq, or Kuwait. I'd already spent far too many of the seventeen million minutes of my life in hellholes where the temperature rarely dropped below ninety.

"Can we just pretend for a little while?"

"What's that?"

"That this, right here, is our whole world. No terrorists, no missions, no guns, no killing, no fucked-up evil-as-shit world leaders. Just the beach, the sand, the water, the island."

"I'm down."

"Thanks, Dutch."

I turned to my side and propped my head on my bent arm. "What's up, Miss Malin?"

"Nothing new. I'm just…tired of it all."

"I was just thinking that myself."

"Yeah?" she asked, turning on her side too.

"I was thinking about what it would take to make me call it quits. Meaning retire for good."

"And?"

"A message from Doc that he needed me to go back to the Middle East—pretty much anywhere. What about you?"

"I had already decided the mission I was working on would be my last."

"For the agency, or in general?"

"Are you asking if I would do what you did and go private?"

I winked. "Don't make it sound so dirty, pretty girl."

She laughed. "Whatever. My answer is no. When I'm done, I'm done." She looked out at the water. "Although I may already be, whether it's my decision or not."

"Why are you so certain the agency wants to burn you?"

She lay back flat on the sand. "I don't know."

"You must have some idea, or you wouldn't think it was that far gone."

She sat up and looked at me. "What do you think, Dutch? I mean you blew up an op I'd been working on for over a year, killed my asset, and kidnapped me from Pakistan, essentially blowing any chance I had of completing the mission the CIA has invested thousands of dollars in."

"Orlov was your asset?"

"Fuck," I heard her say under her breath before she flopped back down on the sand. "We were working together, okay? Wouldn't have been the first time he worked with the agency or even the high-and-mighty K19, would it?"

"High and mighty?"

"Fuck," she mumbled the expletive a second time. "I say ten things, and what do you pick up on?"

"The Orlov thing is kind of a big deal. What were you working on with him?"

Malin laughed. "Wham, bam, thank you, ma'am, and just like that, Dutch Miller returns to the folds of K19 as the conquering hero."

I shook my head. "Wow. I knew you had a low opinion of me, but I had no idea how deep it was."

"Whatever," she said for the third or fourth time, standing and brushing the sand off her legs. "I guess I'll see you later, Dutch. Whether I want to or not."

"What happened to pretending? What happened to this, right here, being our whole world?"

"Sorry, sometimes dreams are short-lived, aren't they?"

"Wait a minute—"

"Fuck off, Dutch."

I watched her run off toward the murderous hills that led back up to the house, in no hurry to follow. In fact, I'd take my damn time and walk back up when I was good and ready.

I wondered if her jab about short-lived dreams related to me and Alegria or to me and her. If it were the latter, Malin likely meant that her own dreams had been short-lived, making me feel, once again, like the absolute shithead asshole I was.

# 8

*Malin*

An hour passed before I heard Dutch come into the house, whistling the only damn song he ever did—Otis Redding's "Sittin' on the Dock of the Bay."

He wasn't that good at carrying a tune, but after hearing it hundreds of times, it was recognizable.

Maybe I'd been too hard on him, but did he really think he could just ask me what Orlov and I had been working on and I'd tell him?

Did he really think I was that stupid? Or that he was that hot? Because neither was the case. If his plan was to keep me here until I told all, we'd be here a damn long time. Considering what was waiting for me back at headquarters, I'd just as soon put that off for as long as possible.

"What?" I said when he knocked on the door. I'd holed myself up in the smallest of the four bedrooms I came across after finding the clothing that Onyx, or whoever, had purchased for me upstairs in the master on the third floor.

I had no intention of sleeping in there, though, with or without Dutch. Not only was this room the smallest, it was also the farthest away.

"There are a couple of things I want to get straight."

"This oughta be good." I twirled the seagrass angel ornament in my hand and tried my hardest not to look at him. If I did, there was a good chance I'd lose my resolve.

Dutch shook his head. "That's one. The attitude. I'm trying to *help* you, so you can drop that shit."

"What else?"

"Don't tell me to fuck off. I don't talk to you that way."

"I didn't kidnap you."

Dutch stalked over to the bed and, before I realized what he was doing, grabbed me by the back of the neck.

"I didn't kidnap you. I saved your life, Malin. You may think Orlov wouldn't have killed you right then, but he would've eventually, just as soon as he'd gotten everything out of you that he wanted."

"How do you know, Dutch? Is that your plan too?"

He wrenched his hand away as though my flesh had burned him, looked into my eyes, shook his head, and stormed out of the room, slamming the door behind him.

Maybe I went a little too far with that last comment, but was he really that oblivious to how mad I was?

Didn't he know that he'd ripped my fucking heart out of my chest and left it in his kitchen that night? How could he think I wouldn't lash out at him, especially when he goaded me?

I closed my eyes and rested my back against the bed's headboard, took a couple of deep breaths, got up, went down one flight of stairs, and found Dutch in the kitchen, pouring a shot of bourbon that didn't look like his first.

"Listen, I'm sorry. I didn't mean that."

Dutch tossed back the shot and poured another. "It doesn't matter."

"It does. I went too far. You know I don't really think you'd ever hurt me, Dutch. Not physically anyway."

"That's it." He slammed the glass down on the counter and walked out the back door.

"Where are you going?" I ran after him when I saw the same boat we'd come over on approaching the dock.

Dutch didn't acknowledge that he heard me, nor did he hesitate to jump on the boat as soon as it was close enough for him to do so.

He and Onyx exchanged a few words before Onyx climbed out of the boat, and Dutch pulled away from the dock.

"Hold up," Onyx hollered at me when I turned to run back up the trail.

There was no reason for me to be so nasty to Onyx just because I was pissed at Dutch. "Is he coming back?" I asked when he got closer.

"I don't know."

"Did he say why he's leaving?"

"Nope, but Dutch doesn't ask for anything he doesn't need, so if he needed to get off this island less than eight hours after arriving, I gotta think something serious happened."

"I asked if he was going to kill me after he got the information he wanted out of me."

"Seriously? I mean, were you serious?"

"At the time."

Onyx whistled and shook his head. "Damn, Malin. Were you tryin' to rip the guy's heart out?"

Interesting choice of words on Onyx's part because, maybe, that was exactly what I'd been trying to do. Tit for tat as it were. Instead of an eye for an eye, a heart for a heart.

"Are you staying?"

"Do you think Dutch would let me leave you here on your own?"

"We could both leave."

Onyx eyed the bottle of bourbon and the broken glass on the counter. I'd raced after Dutch so fast I hadn't realized it broke when he slammed it down.

Onyx opened cupboards until he found two more. "I prefer it on the rocks. You?"

"Neat, thanks."

He poured two fingers and handed me the glass before he put ice in his.

He motioned for me to follow him out to the deck.

"Why don't you tell me what happened between you and him?" he asked once we were both seated.

"It's a short story."

"Good, then, we can get on to the next one faster."

"Do I really need to say it? Doesn't everyone affiliated with K19 already know?"

"Do I strike you as the kind of man who would bother asking a question I already know the answer to?"

I shrunk down a little bit, if only in my head. Onyx was pretty damn intimidating when he puffed himself up like that. "No," I muttered.

"Now, tell me what happened."

"Alegria called, and he went running to her."

Onyx nodded. "That's the short version. Now tell me the long one."

"Why would I do that?"

"Have you told anyone?"

I shook my head.

"Then, it's about damn time you got it off your chest."

I told him everything, right down to my pink panties and the fact that only thirty minutes before the woman called, Dutch had given me the best orgasm of my life.

"And just like that"—I snapped my fingers—"he was gone. Didn't even wait to walk me to my car."

Onyx shook his head. It wasn't the first time he did in the course of my story.

"That explains why you asked if he planned to kill you."

"It does?"

"What Dutch did to you was about the worst thing you could ever imagine, wasn't it?"

I nodded.

"So you said the worst thing you could imagine."

"It might be an oversimplification, but I guess so."

"Now, I've got a story to tell you."

"Would you like something to eat?"

"You got any of Sofia's food left?"

"We have all of it."

"I figured Dutch would've polished it all off by now."

"He didn't have time. First, we went for a run, although not together, and then right after he got back, he called you and left."

"I could go for some of that," Onyx said, standing to help me get it all out of the refrigerator.

"You said you had a story to tell me."

Onyx nodded. "I've known Dutch a long time. Not as long as some of the other guys have, but long enough to have seen him transition from who he was when I met him to who he is now."

I dished some food onto a plate to reheat in the microwave.

"You know," he said. "Some of us grow up quicker than others."

I laughed.

"Dutch…he lived in the past for a long while. From the day I met him, I knew he had a thing for Alegria, not that it made any sense to me."

I took my plate out when the microwave dinged, put Onyx's in, and sat at the counter.

"It was kind of like watching someone with a celebrity."

I rolled my eyes, and Onyx laughed.

"Just that they hung out and all, but it was more like he was in love with the idea of the woman rather than the woman herself."

"He went from my bed to hers pretty damn quick."

"I'm not saying anything he did was right. I just know that when the opportunity presented itself for him to have something he'd wanted for so long, he didn't think with the right part of his anatomy."

"If this is supposed to make me feel better, it isn't."

"All I'm saying is that I think he gets it now."

"Now that she's with Mantis."

Onyx sat beside me at the kitchen island and shoveled food in faster than I'd even seen Dutch do.

"No, it was before that. The reason Dutch was in Germany was because he begged Doc for a mission—any mission. He walked away to give his two best friends in the world the chance to get their shit together and figure out they were made for each other."

Onyx stood and walked back over to where the containers of food were still on the counter. "Want some more?"

"I'm good." I took my plate to the sink.

"Mantis told me that when he rescued him from the pirates in Somalia, one of the first things Dutch asked was if he wanted him to back away."

"And?"

"Mantis said no, but Dutch did it anyway."

"How noble of him."

"Listen, Malin, Mantis got it wrong. Dutch saw that and gave him the push he needed to make it right. If Alegria had refused to listen to him, there would be two more miserable people in the world instead of two happy ones."

"I'm not sure what you're trying to tell me. Dutch is a great guy. I get that. However, he wasn't that great of a guy to me. I'm entitled not to think he's the prince of a man everyone else thinks he is."

"You are, but consider this. What if you listen to him when he tells you how sorry he is? How about if you consider that he didn't have to do any of this? He's acting on instinct alone, Malin. He believes you're in danger, and he went to K19 and asked the team to help him. Not only that, he offered to fund all of this himself. He didn't have to do that either."

"I didn't ask him to."

"I know you didn't."

I knew Onyx was getting frustrated with me, but what was the point in us talking if I couldn't be honest about how I felt?

"Dutch did it all anyway. Despite the fact that you didn't ask for help. Look at it that way for a minute. How many people insist that someone accept their help when the personal cost to themselves is so great?"

It was on the tip of my tongue to repeat that I hadn't asked for Dutch's help, but I got the point Onyx was trying to make.

"Only someone who really cares. That's who," he added when I didn't say anything.

"He's gone now, so I guess I'm on my own. I'll contact Copeland tomorrow and make arrangements to get back to headquarters."

# 9

*Dutch*

I'd never, not once, walked away from a mission. Maybe the reason I did earlier was because, to me, it wasn't one. I was saving Malin's life. That wasn't a mission. Something in my gut told me whatever she was caught up in, was that serious.

I cared for her. Deeply. She was a woman I might fall in love with if I believed in that sort of thing anymore. At one time, I thought I loved Alegria, but now that I knew better, I doubted I'd ever be capable of feeling the emotion.

A few hours ago, I told myself that if I had to do it over again, I wouldn't do anything differently that night that I left Malin for the woman who would soon be Mantis' wife, but I changed my mind.

If I could go back in time, I'd take Malin with me when Alegria called, drunk, begging me to come to her. Instead of choosing her over Malin, the two of us would've brought Alegria back to my house, let her sleep it off, and then helped her figure out her shit with Mantis once and for all. Hindsight, right?

One thing I was certain of, if I could have a do-over, I wouldn't have had sex with Alegria, not even once. The other thing I'd do would be to pull my head out of my ass and realize how amazing Malin was before it was too late.

"I'll have whatever he's having," said the last voice I expected to hear as I sat at the bar drowning my sorrows.

"What are you doing here, Doc?"

"I got a call from Onyx."

"That bastard."

"Now, now. He must've had a good reason since he asked me to fly down here."

I lowered my head. "God, Doc. I'm sorry. I just needed to get out of there for a little while."

"What happened?"

I downed the shot the bartender set in front of me. "Where'd you fly in from?"

"Reagan."

"I thought you would've gone home by now."

"I was headed there."

"Shit."

"I think you've had enough," Doc said when I motioned for the bartender to pour me another round.

If anyone else did that, I would've taken their head off, but not with Doc. There wasn't a man in the world I respected more than the one sitting next to me.

I pushed my empty glass away.

"What's next?" Doc asked.

"What do you mean?"

"Are you done?"

"I think we both know I've had too much to drink."

"I'm talking about Malin."

I scratched my chin. I didn't know what I wanted to do about the lovely Miss Malin.

"She hit hard."

"She hit back."

"I know."

"An extreme reaction on your part."

"Me leaving? Yeah, I had to."

"Tell me why."

"What are you, Doc, a psychiatrist now too?"

"Nope," he answered, shaking his head. "I'm just a friend."

"It hurt," I mumbled.

Doc didn't say anything.

"Everything she said to me today hurt. One minute she was asking if we could pretend that living on the island was our life, and then the next, she was asking if I was going to kill her."

"Harsh."

"When she apologized—if you could call it that—she said she knew I'd never hurt her, at least not physically."

"Sounds like the two of you have unfinished business."

"What am I supposed to do, just let her hurl that unfinished shit at me whenever she feels like it?"

"You know what to do," Doc responded, standing and pushing his barstool in. "I'm going home to my wife and baby boy."

"I envy you, Doc."

"Then, do something about it."

"I don't think it's in the cards for me."

Doc patted my back before he walked away. "Bullshit."

# 10

*Malin*

"The hell you will."

Onyx and I jumped when Dutch spoke from just inside the kitchen door, obviously having overheard my plan to contact Cope and return to headquarters in the morning.

"I may not be the person you want to help you with this, and you may not want to admit even to yourself how deep the shit is you're in, but I'm not going to let you walk in front of a firing squad. You tell me who you want to talk to, who you want here, and I'll make it happen."

"Perfect timing," said Onyx, dropping his dishes in the sink and wiping his hands on a paper towel. "I was just telling Malin I need to get back for a flight, so if I'm done here, I'll head down to the boat."

Onyx didn't bother looking at me, but walked out the door when Dutch nodded.

"Are you hungry?" I asked, avoiding everything he'd just said, even if only to give myself a chance to breathe before he and I got into it again.

"Always," he grunted.

I waved my hand over the food Sofia had made. "This okay?"

"It'll do."

I looked up at him.

"I'm more in the mood for spaghetti and meatballs."

I smiled when he winked.

"Listen, Dutch—"

"Let's not jump right in yet, okay?"

"Of course." I turned around to put his plate in the microwave and took another deep breath.

There was so much left unsaid between us. I made a vow to myself not to keep dropping f-bombs on him. When we were both ready, we needed to sit down and talk. If he wasn't ready right now, I'd be happy to wait.

The truth was, I missed Dutch and not just the physical part of our relationship. Sure, the man was scorchingly hot, but he was also fun to be around, smart, and we always had something to talk about. When neither of us felt like talking, we could do quiet too. I couldn't remember a time when things were awkward between us before *Alegria-fucking-geddon*, not from the first time we were together.

That night had been everything I'd dreamed of up until that point in my life.

\* \* \*

"Tell me you want this as much as I do," Dutch said as he pushed me up against the passenger door of his car.

I told him I did, but God, it was so much more than that. I'd wanted him an hour after I met him. There were times when we'd be in meetings and he'd ask me a question and then scrunch his eyes like he was wondering what I was thinking about.

Every time, what I was thinking was the same—what he'd look like if he took off that crisp white button-down shirt he wore every day and the t-shirt he wore under it. I'd imagine that we were the only two people in the room, and that when I walked over and loosened his tie, he'd pull me onto his lap so I was straddling him. My fantasies only got hotter from there. Had I wanted this? More than I'd ever wanted anything in my life.

He lifted me, taking my mouth in a mind-blowing kiss when I wrapped my legs around his waist.

"I like these," he groaned, sliding his fingers inside my short shorts. "But I'd like them better off of you."

I wrapped my legs tighter around him so his hardness pressed against my sex.

"I can't wait. I need to see your gorgeous tits. Show me."

With shaking hands, I slid both straps of my camisole off my shoulders and down my arms until my nipples popped out. My whole body buzzed with want, and when he leaned forward and licked me, I almost orgasmed then.

I arched my back and sparks of heat shot straight through my core.

"God, you taste good," he said, moving to the other nipple. When I felt his bite of pain, I had my first climax at the hands and mouth of Dutch Miller.

"Jesus," he moaned. "I'd take you here and now if I hadn't waited so long for this."

"What? You waited? For this?" My head was spinning so fast, I thought I was imagining his words.

"Look at me," he demanded. "Since the very first day we met."

"Me too."

Dutch slid me down his body and then pulled me away from the car so he could open the door. When I moved to get in, he grabbed my arm and pulled me back to him, giving me another of his mind-blowing kisses.

"I won't be able to drive with you looking like this," he said, pulling the straps of my camisole back up to my shoulders. "As much as I'd like to tell you to take this off." He plucked at the strap. "And these." He tugged at my shorts. "And have you naked next to me, I'd much rather take my time, have you in my bed, naked for as long as you'll let me keep you there."

Dazed, I got in the car and waited for him to get in the other side.

He reached around me, grabbed the seat belt, and fastened it while, at the same time, running his tongue across my exposed skin. His tongue teased the lobe of my ear.

"I know how much you want me, Malin. Do you know what that does to me? Do you know how hard it is to wait?"

I closed my eyes and whimpered when he cupped my sex with his palm.

"I am going to fuck you so hard for so long, you won't even remember your name." He shifted back into the driver's seat and started the engine.

While the ride to his house was short, it seemed endless as I sat beside him, a quivering mass of need.

"Wait," he said, pulling into the driveway. He got out, came around to my side, opened my door, and pulled me with him.

My cheeks flushed and my eyes glazed as I waited impatiently for him to open the front door.

Once inside, he didn't hesitate. Within seconds my camisole was off and lying somewhere on the floor. He knelt in front of me and pulled my shorts off over my hips.

"Oh my God," he groaned. "Are you telling me you weren't wearing panties?"

I nodded.

"I almost lost it right then, woman."

When Dutch kissed across my bare skin, I wove my fingers in his hair.

"Dutch, please," I moaned, willing him to stand and fuck me right there in his kitchen. Instead, he took one of my legs and rested it over his shoulder as he devoured my pussy until I could no longer stand.

When I felt my legs giving way, Dutch finally stood, swept me into his arms, and carried me up a flight of stairs. He set me on his bed, walked over, and turned on the light that sat on his bedside table.

His eyes never left my body while he shed his clothes, donned a condom, and moved over me, catching one of my nipples for a quick bite before moving up to ravage my mouth again.

I tried to move enough that I could get him to fill the ache between my legs, but he stopped kissing me and shook his head.

"You're mine now, Malin," he repeated the words he'd said earlier when we were leaving the bar. "I'll do what I want, when I want, and you, my beauty, must wait."

I shook my head, ready to cry with how on edge I was, how much I longed to feel him inside me, but he didn't hurry. He slowly made his way down my body with his tongue until finally, finally he moved enough that his cock pressed against my pussy.

He stopped and looked into my eyes. "How many times have you imagined what this would feel like?"

"Hundreds," I moaned, grabbing him and trying to push him closer.

"Thousands for me." He kissed me, thrusting his tongue into my mouth.

"Look at me," he demanded, and when I did, he slowly entered me. "I don't ever want to forget this moment, finally knowing what it feels like to be inside you." He thrust harder. "It feels so much better than I dreamed it would."

As much as I longed for him to move inside me, the idea that we were both so focused on how it felt to finally have our bodies joined, brought me to another climax.

\* \* \*

I looked up when I heard the microwave ding; Dutch was studying me. I cleared my throat, took the plate out, and set it in front of him.

"Would you like something to drink?" My voice cracked when I said it.

"Nope," he said, shaking his head. "But, Malin"—he waited until I looked at him—"I think about it all the time too."

# 11

*Dutch*

I knew what she was thinking about. It was written all over her features. Her nipples were pebbled, and the flush in her face had spread down her neck. Even if she didn't realize it, I did. The same thing I thought about all the time—the first night we were together.

"I'll be right back." She rushed out of the kitchen and ran up the stairs.

Sex between us had been off the charts from the very first time. Her body responded to mine like no other woman's ever had, and maybe because of that—or just because she was so damn hot—my body did the same.

Ten minutes after taking both of us over the edge, I'd find myself ready to take her again, and she'd be ready too.

It wasn't just the sex, though. It never had been. I liked Malin. A lot. Whenever she'd spend the weekend at my place, I felt the loss of her, her company, everything about her, when she had to leave.

I always made her promise to text me when she got home, and each time she did, I'd beg her to come back. More than once, she surprised me and showed up at my door thirty minutes later, making me feel like a man who had just won the lottery.

I rarely went to her place, mainly because there were too many other agents living in her building. I wouldn't have minded if they knew we were together, but she would've, and I respected that.

There were times, though, when I longed to just show up at her door, beg her to let me in, and then refuse to ever leave.

Until that horrible, stupid night when Alegria called. It was like the screech of a car in a cartoon; that's how drastic of an end it was for my relationship with Malin. When I closed my eyes and thought about it now, playing back the memory felt like watching a train wreck. There wasn't a single moment in my life I regretted more than that one.

I'd known she was getting dressed, that she'd be out in under five minutes, but I'd left anyway. Not so much because I was in a hurry, but more, I wouldn't have known what to say to her. Should I have said goodbye?

Or maybe tried to tell her something about Alegria? I didn't know the answer better now than I did then.

It dawned on me that she was still gone. Probably had no intention of being "right back," so I went looking for her.

I found her in the same small second-floor bedroom where she'd been earlier, but this time I didn't knock.

I stalked over to the bed where she sat with her back against the headboard. She was clutching her seagrass angel while tears streamed down her cheeks. Instead of sitting beside her, I put my arm under her legs and around her waist, picked her up, and carried her upstairs.

Malin didn't protest, or even speak; she rested her head on my shoulder and wrapped her arms around my neck.

I didn't let go when we got to the top of the stairs. Instead, I sat down and held her on my lap, my grip around her tight.

"Letting you go was the worst mistake of my life. As much as you'll never forgive me for it, is how much I'll never forgive myself."

"You hurt me...so bad..." she whispered.

"I know I did. Believe me, if there were ever a way for me to take that pain away from you, I would."

"I want to forgive you. I want to forget, but I can't. I wish I could."

"I know, baby, and I'm not asking you to. I know what I did is something we can never get past."

Malin cried harder, and I tightened my grip. "Let it out," I said. "Let it all out."

"You were all I ever wanted," she said a few minutes later.

I bent my neck and looked up at the ceiling. I'd suffer every second of regret, knowing I deserved it. Whatever she had to say, I'd listen and remember, knowing I'd earned every bit of the castigation she meted out.

"I know saying I'm sorry will never be enough."

She buried her face in the crook of my neck, dampening my shirt with her tears.

"I'll say it to you every day, for as many days as you'll let me, and hope that one day you can forgive me."

Malin pulled back so I could see her tear-stained face and look into her sad eyes.

Dare I? Should I? Whatever the answer, I couldn't stop myself. When she looked at my mouth, I brought it to hers. My kiss was tentative. It was Malin who pushed against my lips with her tongue until they opened to her.

I grabbed the back of her head and held her close, thrusting my tongue in her mouth, grazing her teeth with mine, nipping at her lip until I tasted the faint metallic flavor of blood. I pulled back, not wanting to hurt her, but she wouldn't let me. She came back at me, fusing our mouths together as she pulled my tucked-in shirt out of my pants.

"Wait," I said, catching her hands with mine. "Are you sure about this?"

Malin's fingers tightened their grip. "If you reject me now, Dutch, I'll walk out the door, and you'll never see me again."

"Baby," I said, stroking her face with my fingers. "I want you so bad, I just want you to be sure."

"Let's just pretend," she whispered, pulling my shirt up and over my stomach. I helped, taking it over my head and tossing it on the floor.

When I saw her hands on the hem of her own shirt, I rested mine on top of them. "Let me," I begged; Malin nodded.

I took my time removing her clothes, letting my eyes linger on every naked inch of her skin. Her body was perfect. Toned from her extraordinary level of fitness, yet still soft, still curvy, like a woman should be.

I trailed my lips everywhere, stopping for seconds that dragged on to minutes as my body learned hers all over again.

She moaned and writhed, pleaded and pulled at me, but I wouldn't hurry.

When I got done, there could be no question in Malin's mind that I worshiped her. When I tried to move her arm away from her body, to run my tongue over the arrow tattoos I loved so much, she tensed and wouldn't let me.

"Let me see," I said, easing her arm from her side.

What I saw there came close to breaking me. Instead of two arrows, there were three. The third tattoo was of an arrow piercing a heart.

I felt it as though an arrow had pierced my own. That is what I'd done to her. I'd put an arrow straight through her heart. Rather than moving her arm back, hiding her pain, I ran my tongue over the newest tattoo.

"Forgive me," I said, tracing its detail. "Please forgive me."

"Make love to me, Dutch."

I took a deep breath. "Baby, I want you more than anything, but we can't."

She pulled back and looked into my eyes.

"I don't have any condoms."

"I have an IUD. I've had it since we were together."

I kept my eyes focused on hers. "I haven't…" I couldn't bring myself to say it. I wanted her to know that I'd only been with Alegria and I'd used a condom every time, but I couldn't say it. Not now. I couldn't mention another woman's name when I had Malin in my arms.

While I hesitated, trying to figure out what to do, Malin moved away from me. I watched as her hands came to my belt, loosened it, and then opened my zipper. She put her hands under me, and I lifted, helping her pull my pants from my body. When they were off, she pushed my shoulders back and straddled me.

I brought my hands to her tits and then to her hips, helping as she eased onto my cock.

Once she was seated, I swear my eyes rolled back in my head. When she started to move, I knew I wouldn't last more than a couple of minutes. I grabbed her hips to stop her, rolled us both over, and took her at a pace I could control.

I kissed her like I used to. Soft at first and then more demanding. Pulling back to nip her lip and then soothing the bite with my tongue.

I remembered how every inch of her felt, as though it was yesterday that our bodies were one.

There were so many things I wanted to say. I wanted her to know how much I'd missed her. How good it felt to have her in my arms again. How nothing had ever felt as right as this did, but I couldn't say any of those things for fear it would bring her hurt back to the surface.

"Dutch?"

"Yeah, baby," I said while scattering kisses all over her.

"Tell me what you're thinking." It was as though she'd read my thoughts.

"Malin...I..."

She put her hands on my shoulders. "Look at me."

I did.

"Are you thinking about me, or her?"

"You. All you," I said, knowing now that I'd made a mistake by withholding my thoughts from her.

I moved inside her slowly and kept my gaze riveted to hers.

"I'm thinking about how much I missed you, this, us. How nothing—no one—ever felt as right as you do. I'm thinking that as long as it's been, as much as I could never have hoped this could ever be, I finally feel as though I'm exactly where I should be, with the exact person I want to be with. I'm thinking that this is home, Malin. Wherever you are, as long as we're together, it's home."

When I moved faster, thrust deeper, she dug her fingernails into my shoulders.

At some point in the night, Malin turned so her back was to my front. My arms remained wrapped around her, my favorite way to sleep. My hardness, because I was always in that state when I was with her, was nestled between the sweet cheeks of her ass while I cuddled her to me, watching over her, protecting her as she slept.

Sleeping with Malin beside me, joining our bodies together, laughing with her when we sneaked back to the kitchen, naked, to get another bowlful of Sofia's delicious food—this was all the good stuff in life, right here. *Malin Kilbourne.*

When I opened my eyes, the sun shone through the window, and I was in bed alone. Neither made me happy. I could easily sleep a few more hours, but without Malin next to me, it wasn't about to happen. Where was she, and why hadn't I woken up when she got out of bed?

Moments later I heard the patter of her feet as the smell of coffee wafted into the room with her.

"This is heaven," I said, pulling her close to me when she crawled back in bed. "You and coffee; there's nothing more a man could ask for."

"This house is pretty nice too." She took a sip of her steamy brew.

"What do you want to do today?" I asked.

"That run felt pretty great yesterday."

"There were many things that felt great to me yesterday, and none of them were that run."

Malin put her hand on my stomach. "Stick with me, old man, and I'll get you back in shape."

I laughed, but she was right. It had been a long time since I remembered struggling with a workout as much as I did yesterday. "How's the weather look?"

"Perfect. Sunny, but not too warm."

"I hate to ask, but what time is it?"

"Does it matter?"

I smiled. "Sure doesn't."

"We're pretending this is our life, remember? We don't live by a clock."

"I like this life, Malin."

"I do too."

"Look," she said, pointing to something in the trees near the shore after our run.

I followed her over and saw two kayaks, flipped upside down.

"Think they're seaworthy?"

They looked almost brand new. "One way to find out."

I flipped the first over and saw there was a paddle and life vest on the ground underneath it. I lifted it over my head and carried it near the water's edge and went back to get the second one.

"I can help," Malin said, but didn't make a move to.

"Oh, yeah?"

"Yeah. I mean I can, but I'd rather watch you do it."

I walked over to her with the second kayak hoisted over my head, leaned forward, and planted a kiss on her lips. "There are things I like watching you do too."

She smiled. "Like what?"

"Let's see…everything. Preferably without clothes on."

"I'm down with that."

I set the kayak on the sand. "You are?"

"Sure. I'd prefer you without clothes on too."

I looked over at the kayaks and then back at her.

"Not that, though."

I threw my head back and laughed, relieved that she didn't want me to go out in the sound naked. Although for her, I probably would've.

The water level on this side of the island was lower than on the side the dock was on, or rather, the bottom of the sound hadn't been dredged as much on this side. There were times we got stuck and had to push our way off with the paddles.

We kayaked past beaver dams, saw loons, ospreys, and eagles, and then turned back when the sky clouded up and rain threatened.

It was sprinkling when we got back to the shore, and I could hear thunder in the distance. The rain's intensity quickly increased.

"Let's find cover." I held Malin's hand as we ran under a canopy of trees and huddled beneath it.

"We should try to make it back to the house."

"Not a good idea. The lightning is getting closer. I think there's a shed on this side of the island. You wait here, and I'll see if I can find it."

Malin smiled.

"What?"

"You're such an alpha sometimes."

"Sometimes?"

She laughed. "I'm not a girly-girl, Dutch. I never have been. I can go out in the rain. I won't melt."

I couldn't explain why the need to protect her surged through my veins, but it did, and what was wrong with that? How was it different than opening a door for her, or carrying heavy groceries, or any other gentlemanly thing she would accept without giving me shit about it?

"My mother raised me to be a gentleman," I finally said.

"You've never talked about your parents. Any family really."

"No, I don't."

"Why not?"

The further I could distance myself from the memories of my childhood, the happier I was. I preferred not to think about it at all, and I liked talking about it even less, but if I wanted Malin to forgive me—trust me—I needed to do what I wanted her to do, and talk.

"My father died when I was a little kid, and my mother remarried."

"Is that it?"

"Pretty much."

"Siblings?"

"Stepsisters."

"Okay, then. Subject closed."

"It wasn't a good situation."

"I take it you didn't get along with your mother's second husband or his daughters."

Didn't get along? That was one way to put it. More like I could never do a fucking thing right, and when I messed up, I got closely acquainted with the asshole's fists.

"You already know my story," she said, and I did.

She was an only child, raised by her father, whom she had been close to before he died. Her mother left when she was three years old, and Malin had only seen her one time since, when she showed up for her dad's funeral and Malin asked that the woman be escorted out. Her father had never remarried, and consequently, she had no step- or half-siblings.

"My stepfather ruled with an iron fist. At least with me," I said, surprising myself.

"What about your mother? Did he abuse her?"

"No." I would've killed him if he had. "She took his side, though."

"You went to the Air Force Academy."

"That's right."

I still remembered walking to the bus stop alone the day I left home. I hadn't looked or ever gone back.

Fortunately, a family who lived near the academy had "sponsored" me like so many of the local residents did.

In most cases, the cadets spent time with the family more often when they were freshmen and had very limited privileges, but in my case, I remained close to them all four years.

Both the man and the woman, Steve and Mary, were in their sixties when I met them; their children were grown and had lives of their own but visited their parents often.

Steve had been a pilot in the Air Force and had served in the Korean and Vietnam wars. He held the record for parachuting out of a plane that had been shot down, and living through it. Four times he'd gone back and gotten in another plane after being rescued and recovering from whatever injuries he had sustained.

He and Mary had met at church, back in her hometown in Minnesota. Steve had been stationed nearby, and she loved to tell the story of the first day she saw him, when he walked in with his leather jacket and white scarf. Mary's mother had been aghast that the man hadn't worn a coat and tie to mass, but Mary hadn't cared. To her, he was the most handsome man alive.

The two had a good life together, traveling the world and raising their family. When Steve retired, he bought a piece of land with a view of the academy and built Mary her dream house.

I'd known them for ten years when Mary passed away, and Steve followed shortly thereafter. While I knew their children, we'd never been especially close, so I lost touch with them.

My time at the academy would've been much different had I not known Steve and Mary. They always made sure I felt welcome on the weekends and at the holidays. They celebrated my birthday and always had gifts for me then and at Christmas.

"What are you thinking about?"

"The Heilmans. My cadet sponsor family."

"Tell me about them."

I told her everything I'd just thought about, feeling bad at the end that I thought of them so rarely now when they'd once been a lifeline for me.

"I think Steve was disappointed when I didn't get a pilot slot, but he never said anything about it."

"Did any of their children join the military?"

I shook my head. "That probably disappointed him too. Not Mary, though. As the wife of a man who had been shot out of a plane four times, she made no secret that she supported her son's and daughter's decisions to choose careers where they stayed out of harm's way."

"They sound very nice."

"They were the best. I remember that Steve's favorite drink was a *Cuba Libre*, and he'd have a fit if anyone served it to him with spiced rum. And Mary loved her scotch—red label."

Malin laughed. "Were they heavy drinkers?"

"Not at all. It's just that they were both so particular about it. Oh, the other thing about Mary is, one of her favorite things to tell people was that she used to babysit Bob Dylan. She always called him Bobby."

"You miss them."

"I do, and I feel bad that I don't think of them more often."

"We're both orphans. I mean, I am. Is your mother still alive?"

"She is, but I haven't talked to her in years."

"And yet, when I teased you about treating me like a girl, your first response was that she raised you to be a gentleman."

Malin was right; however, I didn't feel like diving too deeply into whatever Freud might think that meant.

"Looks like it's going to clear up," I said, motioning to the patches of blue sky that peeked through the clouds. The rain tapered off, and I'd stopped listening for thunder. "Should we head back?"

When Malin stood and stretched, the shirt she wore rode up, exposing her tummy. I leaned forward and kissed her belly button. I put my hand on her ass and nuzzled my face into her. She put one hand on my shoulder and the other in my hair.

"I like this life, Malin. I like being able to put my hands on you. I hope you like it too."

# 12

## *Malin*

Like it? It was every dream I'd ever had of Dutch come true. While I'd just told him I wasn't a girly-girl, when I was with him, I felt all woman. I'd teased him about being out of shape, but the man was far from it.

His sinewy physique was rock hard, and when his arms were around me, I felt safer than I had since I was a little girl and my father promised to slay my dragons and keep the monsters from under my bed.

Dutch would slay my dragons too. Whether I asked him to or not.

Should I ask him, though? Should I tell him how I wasn't just afraid, I was terrified of what was going to happen to me when the powers that be found out what I'd uncovered? It would mean telling him things I hadn't even told Sergei, who had found out enough of it on his own.

The dragons and monsters would soon be beckoning; I felt it in my bones. I'd gotten used to slaying them on my own, but this time, they would come in a force so strong that even with Dutch's help, I doubted I could overcome them.

"What's on your mind, Malin?" He stood and took his hands off my body. "Is this too much?"

I put my arms around his waist and rested my head against his chest. "Not at all. I don't like our pretend life; I love it. It's just that there will come a time when the pretending will end, and I'll be forced to face real life. I'd rather keep it at bay a while longer."

"No reason to stop pretending today or even tomorrow, is there?"

I smiled. "I'd like to go longer than that."

"Me too, baby," he said before kissing me. "Let's get back to the house and pretend we can't keep our hands off each other."

"That, we don't have to pretend."

"Are you hungry?" I asked when we walked in the house.

"Always, but right now, it isn't for food."

"Good." I led him by the hand toward the staircase.

"Let's stay here," he said, resisting my pull.

I let Dutch lead me back through the kitchen and to the room that was opened to the piazza on one side and looked out over the sound on the other two.

He moved me so I stood in a place where the sun's rays streamed inside, and drew my shirt with the built-in sports bra over my head. He pushed my shorts down along with the panties. When I stood naked in front of him, he took a step back, grabbed a pillow, and threw it on the floor.

"Here," he said, motioning me in the direct path of the warmth.

When I knelt down, he did the same, but when I tried to remove his shirt, he stopped me.

"Dutch?"

"Shh. I want to look at you, Malin. Can you let me just look at you?"

I stretched my body out on the soft throw, closing my eyes as the sun, combined with his gaze, heated my skin.

"Do you know what you do to me?" he asked. "How you make me feel? How my body reacts to yours?"

I tried to push away the pain of wanting to ask him why he hadn't chosen me, then. Why hadn't I been enough to keep him there that night?

The hurt and anguish I felt were so close to the surface that they burned me from the inside out. I felt too exposed. The sun no longer felt warm; it hurt. Everything hurt.

I opened my eyes, ready to flee, and met Dutch's gaze. He reached out and grabbed my nape, forcing me to look into his eyes.

"What just happened?" he asked.

I shook my head.

"Talk to me. What. Just. Happened?" His voice was firm, but he didn't raise it.

"I can't."

"What?"

"I can't forget."

"What brought it back to you now?"

"Everything you said," I cried. "Why wasn't I enough, Dutch?"

"You were. You always were. I was too stupid to see it."

This time I wrenched away from him, stood, and ran up the stairs, not bothering to grab my clothes. I shut the door of the small bedroom that was my sanctuary when being with Dutch became too much for my fragile heart to handle. I stood with my back against the door and felt the chill of my tears as they trailed down my naked body.

# 13

*Dutch*

Maybe I was wrong not to go after Malin, but what could I say that I hadn't said before. Could I keep apologizing? To me, doing so would begin to feel insincere. I was sorry, but I couldn't go back and change what I'd done. It sucked. I was an asshole. But would backing away from her, never seeing her again, help heal Malin's heart more than being here, trying my best to show her how much I cared?

I leaned forward with my head in my hands, feeling more unsure of myself than I ever remembered in my life. I wasn't the kind of man who second-guessed my decisions. Once I came to one, I stuck by it until the circumstances changed enough for me to reconsider the course I was on.

Was that the case now? Was there a better way for me to get through to Malin? Walking away from her now wasn't something I could do, but would a different approach be better?

I shook my head. And what approach would that be? I was so far out of my element with her, I didn't know if there was an "approach." I just wanted to be with her. Sure, I needed to figure out what she'd gotten herself into with this mission because, whatever it was, it was bad enough for her to believe the CIA would burn her. But that wasn't the main reason I was here. I may have thought it was when we were on the plane, flying back from Bagram, but now I knew better.

The secrets Malin was keeping, served as an excuse for me to take her away, spend time with her, get her to forgive me, and give me another chance. What if I told her exactly that? Would it help if I just laid it all out in front of her?

Instead of trying to manipulate Malin into telling me things she wasn't ready to talk about, what if I was just honest?

I walked up the stairs to the room she'd sequestered herself in and knocked. "Malin, baby, can we talk? There are things I need to tell you."

"Not now, Dutch."

"Yeah, now. We need to do this. For both of us. Put some clothes on and come downstairs when you're ready."

I went back to the kitchen not knowing what to do while I waited.

I'd learned to cook right after I was commissioned in the Air Force; for someone to love to eat as much as I did, I had to. In those days, my second lieutenant pay didn't stretch very far. Egg-white omelets were one of my specialties, not that I made them very often for myself, but they were Malin's favorite. I added dry wheat toast, divvied the food up on two plates, and set both on the table that looked out over the sound.

I sat and waited, not caring if my food got cold. I wouldn't eat until she joined me, even if it took all day for her to be ready to come out.

Less than ten minutes later—not that I was counting minutes or anything—I heard her footfalls. I didn't turn around in my chair even though my back was to her. I sat and waited until she was ready to come and face me.

I almost closed my eyes in relief when she brushed past me. Malin sat in the chair next to me instead of taking the one across the table where I'd set her plate.

"This looks good," she murmured, pulling the food over to her. "Thank you."

"You're welcome."

She ate every bite before she spoke again. "I'm sorry about earlier."

I shook my head. "Don't be."

"I felt…vulnerable. Too…exposed."

"I wanted you to be."

For the first time since she sat down, she looked at me. "Why would you do that to me?"

"The truth?" I asked and didn't wait for her to answer before continuing. "Because I wanted to see if you trusted me."

"That's bullshit."

"Maybe, but it got us there a hell of a lot quicker than if I'd come right out and asked you."

"I didn't like it."

"I know." I leaned forward and rested my hand on her arm. "There are things I should've told you before we left Bagram."

Her eyes opened wide, and she took a deep breath.

"First, don't get any ideas that I know the real objective of your mission. I don't. I only know—knew at the time—that whatever it was, was far more dangerous than you might be willing to admit even to yourself. I haven't even read the brief, Malin."

She nodded, so I kept talking.

"The idea of hiding you, being alone with you, even breaking you down so you'd talk to me, had a lot less to do with your mission than me wanting to be with you again."

"Dutch, I'm—"

"I'm sorry to interrupt you, Malin, but I need to say this. Without giving it a second thought, I manipulated you. Sure, you knew what I was doing, but that didn't stop me from thinking that I could make you do something you didn't want to do."

"Tell you about my mission?"

"That's right, and before you get the idea that Doc or anyone else sent me to Islamabad or convinced me to take you off the grid, they didn't. This is all me, baby."

"I think I knew that, or I did after Onyx told me."

"He's a good guy."

"He is."

"Anyway." I scrubbed my face with my hand. "This is hard."

Her hands were on her lap, but not folded or crossed.

"I want it all, Malin. I want you to lie on the floor, naked, and let me look at you. I want you to tell me where your mission took a wrong turn and what kind of trouble you're really in. I want you to trust me enough to do both of those things, but so much more."

"What more?"

"I don't know, and that's me being honest with you. I don't know what else I'm asking, but I know there's more I want from you than just your trust."

"You wrecked me, Dutch. That's me being honest. You totally, completely annihilated me."

"Why did you tell me to go to her? Why didn't you put up a fight?"

Malin leaned forward, resting her elbows on the table. "To what end? Did you want me to throw away what little pride I had and beg you to pick me over her, knowing full well you wouldn't?"

I shook my head and looked away from her. "I don't know."

"My telling you to go let you off the hook for something you were going to do no matter what. You didn't even wait for me to get dressed."

I cringed. Looking back on it, it had been a chicken-shit-asshole move. "Earlier, when you went up to the bedroom and closed the door, I sat out here not knowing what to do. Maybe it was more that I didn't know what to say. I've apologized to you; I've told you that I wish I could go back and do it all over again. I even wish sometimes that I'd never met Alegria, but the more I say those words, the less authentic they sound to me.

I mean them with all my heart, but I can't keep saying them, because there will come a time when I don't mean them anymore."

I waited for her to speak, but she didn't, so I went on. "Tell me what to do, Malin. Tell me how to make it better or how to make it up to you. Tell me, and I'll do whatever you want. The only thing I can't do is keep saying the same things over again, knowing that it isn't making any difference."

"I don't know what I want you to do."

"Let me ask you this, then. Is it worth it to you to keep trying? Whatever the outcome ends up being, and that includes us just being able to be friends again."

"I don't know."

"Fair enough."

"It is?"

"I guess it's going to have to be."

"Are we leaving the island?"

I rested my elbow on the table like she had and peered into her eyes. "Do you want to?"

"No."

"Then, no. We aren't leaving."

"How long can we stay?"

I thought about it a long time before I answered, wanting to be sure I meant the first words that came to my mind when she asked the question. If I said the words out loud, I had to be sure I was ready to do what it took to make it happen, because once I made her the promise, I would fulfill it, no matter what.

"We can stay here forever, Malin, and I'm not being flip or funny or anything like that. We never have to leave."

She studied me. "How?"

"I'll make it happen."

Her eyes remained fixed on mine, perhaps waiting for a sign that I was bullshitting her.

"What do I have to do?" she asked.

"Not a thing."

"Tell you about the mission?"

"I hope you do, but it isn't a condition of staying here."

"I don't believe you."

"Fair enough," I said for the second time.

"Go to hell, Dutch," she spat and moved her chair to leave, but I grabbed her arm.

"This isn't a joke, Malin. I'm dead serious."

"Why would you do this to me?"

"I'm not doing anything to you."

"You're playing with me, and I don't understand why. Is it so I'll admit I want to be with you? And then what, I have to prove it to you by trusting you?"

"Sit back down."

She hesitated, but then did as I asked.

"I don't want you thinking every time we disagree that we're going to leave. I don't want you thinking you have to leave at all. I want you to just be, Malin. Does that make sense to you? Just...be. No demands, no negotiations. Stop. Breathe. Be."

"What would you do, buy the island?"

I nodded. "I told you I would retire if Doc asked me to take on another mission in the Middle East. Instead of throwing down that gauntlet, I'll just retire now and make this my permanent home."

"How would you be able to afford to buy an island? Never mind, it isn't any of my business."

"I'll tell you how. I saved a hell of a lot of money. I worked damn hard, and never had a reason to spend it. I took my retirement from the Air Force, the money I got when I left the CIA, and what I've made since I became a K19 partner, and invested it. The only significant thing I used the money for was to buy a house in Newport News. With all the work I did to it, it's valued at three times the amount I paid for it. I don't have to do a damn thing for the rest of my life if I don't want to."

"Why are you telling me this?"

"Because you asked."

"And then I said it wasn't my business."

"There isn't anything I'm not willing to share with you, Malin. If you have a question, ask it."

"I only have one question for you."

"Go ahead. Ask."

"Do you still love her?"

"I do. I always will," I answered, looking into Malin's eyes. "But not romantically—as a friend. If anything positive came out of the time I spent with her, it's that I realized I never loved Alegria the way I thought I did. When I met her, I was a kid. I was infatuated, lusted after her, but it wasn't her I was in love with; it was the idea of her. Fantasy and reality were very different."

"I don't want you to buy the island, Dutch."

I nodded, surprised that her saying so hurt a little.

"Maybe someday, but not now. Not for me."

"I understand." I tried not to hang my head. She was saying she didn't want me, and that was okay.

"I don't think you do."

"No? Enlighten me, then."

She laughed. "We've only been here three days."

"It's the perfect pretend place to live, though, isn't it?"

She smiled. "It is. Maybe someday it could be the perfect real place to live."

"I'd really like that, Malin."

"I want to talk business, Dutch."

"Go ahead." I held my breath, not sure I wanted to know what she was about to say.

"I'd like you to read the brief, and if there's anything in it you think I should know, I want you to tell me."

"I can do that."

"Now, Dutch."

I smiled and ran up two flights of stairs to the bedroom where I'd put my laptop. It had been so long since I'd looked at it, I didn't know if it still had a charge. Just in case, I pulled the cord out of my bag too. As I turned to go back down to the kitchen, I saw Malin's angel ornament sitting on the nightstand. I picked it up and took it with me.

"Are you sure you don't want to read it?" I asked, setting the ornament on the counter in front of her.

"Maybe I will. It depends on what you think when you're finished." Malin picked up the angel and dangled it from her finger.

# 14

*Malin*

I would know, just by the look on his face when he read it, whether the brief contained anything significant. I doubted it did, but with the CIA, one could never be sure how much they knew and didn't know.

The chime of the computer starting up signaled, and Dutch waited. I watched as he typed in his credentials, and then waited while he pulled up his email, downloaded the brief, and read it.

When he was finished, he looked at me. "You were investigating Middle Eastern terrorist cells."

"Initially."

"For what purpose initially?"

"I received an alert that a significant amount of money had come into the US and went directly into a Super PAC. This happened right before the election."

"When you say 'right before,' how close to the election are we talking?"

"Less than two weeks."

"By the time it had to be reported, the election was over."

"Exactly."

"Then, what happened?"

"I received another alert that close to the same amount moved out, transferred to a known terrorist organization, leading me to believe that there was a significant strike planned on US soil."

"Ghafor?"

"He was the primary suspect." The Islamic State was definitely in the top three of terrorist organizations that posed the biggest threats to the United States.

Dutch nodded, clearly trying to think this through; however, it would take him miles of thought before he got to the place where I was, if he ever got there at all.

"Listen, I…uh…am I allowed to keep asking questions?"

I covered my smile and did my best not to laugh. Dutch Miller was one of the toughest men I knew, and here he was, walking on eggshells for me.

"Why don't I start at the beginning?"

"Before you begin, can I get something else to eat?"

As hard as I tried, I couldn't contain my laugh. "Of course."

"You think it's funny, but I'm literally starving over here. Aren't you hungry?"

I kept laughing. "You made me breakfast."

"How can you exist on an egg-white omelet and toast? I was hungrier after we finished eating than before."

"I get it, Dutch," I said, squeezing his shoulder and walking into the kitchen. "Is there any of Sofia's food left?"

"I think that's why I'm so hungry. I don't think I've eaten a quarter of it."

"You need to keep your strength up."

Dutch looked up from his computer and smiled. "I do?"

I laughed again.

"What?"

I walked around the kitchen island and stood in front of him. "Sometimes you're like a little boy."

He put his hand on my neck. "And sometimes I'm not." He leaned forward and kissed me. When his tongue pushed through my lips, I put my arms around his neck and kissed him back, harder.

"Oh, God," he groaned, looking up at the ceiling.

"What?"

"I'm so hungry, and yet I want you so bad."

"Let's eat first."

"But then we need to talk too."

"Are you whining?"

Dutch stuck his lower lip out. "I am *so* whining."

# 15

*Dutch*

When Malin went back around the kitchen island to continue heating up food, my phone pinged. I didn't want to look, but knew I had to.

*Malin Kilbourne is on the agency's alert list,* said the text from Doc.

"*Fuck,*" I muttered, wishing it had taken them a few more days to get to this point.

When I looked up, Malin was studying me.

"They're actively looking for you."

She nodded. "What do you know about Ghafor's whereabouts?"

"I'll ask." I sent Doc a message and then set the phone down. "I think we need to move talking up to a higher priority."

*Ghafor's 20's an undisclosed location.*

"Ghafor is still with Striker and whoever else is on the team K19 put together."

Malin nodded. "Is the agency looking for him?"

I sent Doc another text. "Affirmative," I told her a few seconds later.

"So, both of us." Malin tapped her cheek with her fingertip. "Who else is with them?"

I continued texting back and forth with Doc, either confirming or answering the questions Malin fired at me.

"Ask who else specifically, please."

"Monk...shit."

"Who else?"

"Ranger and Diesel."

Instead of freaking out or even looking mildly concerned, Malin just nodded.

"You wanna fill me in on what your reaction means?"

"They were covering Somalia."

"They went in when we did to get Tackle and Halo."

"On the mission with you and Striker."

I nodded.

"We need to find out where they're holding Ghafor."

"No way in hell," I boomed, anticipating what she was about to say. "We are not going wherever they are."

"Then, Doc needs to figure out a way to pull Striker out of there."

"Why?" Maybe it was the lack of food, but I was having a damn hard time following Malin's train of thought.

.

"Because Striker might be in on what I've been investigating."

"We need to talk to Doc."

Malin waited while I sent the message.

"Awesome." I looked at my phone. "He said to give him fifteen."

Malin set a plate in front of me. "Eat up, Miller. We have a lot of work to do." She drummed her fingers on her chin. "Tell Doc we need an hour."

As momentarily hopeful as I was, it only took me an instant to realize she wanted to talk to me about her mission, and that was the only reason we needed more time.

She was grinning again, which meant she knew exactly where my mind had first gone.

"May I?" she asked, motioning to my computer.

I hesitated, surprising myself. Hadn't I been lecturing Malin about her lack of trust in me? Now I was contemplating whether or not to let her use my computer. It was on the tip of my tongue to ask her what she was going to do. Instead, I bit it and spun the laptop around.

"That looked like it was painful."

"Swallowing some of my own medicine."

By the time I'd finished eating, Malin had several windows open on the screen. While she did that, I processed through everything Striker had done and said in Islamabad.

She met my gaze. "We're going to start at the beginning."

"Let's do this."

"As I said, I started out tracking money that came into the Super PAC. At first, I thought whoever brought it in had someone on the inside. Maybe even with Treasury, but Ed Montgomery got wind of what I was working on and assigned me the mission to infiltrate the Islamic State."

I recognized the name. Ed Montgomery was a career agent, old-school type. He should've retired long ago, but the guy kept moving up the ladder, albeit damn slowly. Last I'd heard, Monty was Deputy Director of Congressional Affairs for the CIA. Assigning Malin the mission he did, smelled a lot like he'd been setting her up for a hit.

"Monty is way above your handler, Copeland."

Malin nodded.

"Who was between them?"

"First Striker, and then after he left, McTiernan took his job. Paul Stevens was their boss."

"Stevens. Sounds familiar."

"Deputy Director of NCS."

"Not under Montgomery."

"Nope. Stevens works directly for Flatley."

"What was Monty doing, poking around in National Clandestine Service business? Not to mention, assigning you to a mission. It's way out of his lane."

Malin shrugged. "Interesting you use those words. That was the warning I got. To stay in my lane."

"From Montgomery directly?"

Malin shook her head. "The warning was anonymous."

"You got suspicious."

"Quietly so. It was definitely a mystery."

"What led you to Ghafor?"

"I found something that led me to believe the money was going back out to him."

"What?"

Malin opened up another window on my computer. It was only a screenshot, but it clearly showed three transfers totaling the same amount as the incoming money. All were under the threshold that would raise red flags.

"Wait a minute. You said you received an alert about the money going into the Super PAC."

"That's right."

"And then you said you found something that led you to believe the money went out to Ghafor, but really, you received something leading you to believe it had."

Malin nodded.

"You got both tips from the same person. Who?"

"Someone at DHS."

"Someone you trust?"

"Implicitly."

"Will you tell me who it is?"

Malin shook her head.

I leaned back and put my hands behind my head. "In from God knows who, and then right back out to the Islamic State."

"That's right."

"Talk to me about how all this went from following this money to infiltrating Ghafor's organization."

"They were essentially one and the same, except as I said, I was warned away from the money. The goal was always to bring the Islamic State down by identifying their weaknesses."

"Via infiltration as a trainer for female recruits?"

"Correct."

"So, your stated mission allowed you to mount a different one of your own."

"Yes."

"Where is your Homeland Security contact based?"

"Virginia."

"High-ranking?"

Malin nodded again.

"Male or female?"

She scrunched her eyes. "What difference does that make?"

"Male, then."

"Dutch?"

"Is it someone you've had a relationship with in the past?"

Malin put her hands on her hips. "What the hell?"

"I'm a jealous SOB, baby. It's not something I'll ever apologize for."

"You're joking."

"I'm not."

"Are the questions you asked me about my DHS contact relevant to anything other than your Neanderthal tendencies?"

"Nope."

I waited to see if Malin would tell me more about her mission, or if she was done talking.

"You must have some kind of theory," I said.

Malin had a faraway look in her eyes.

"But you aren't ready to tell me what it is."

"I can't prove it. I can't prove anything other than money came in and then went back out again."

"Your guy at DHS doesn't have anything else for you?"

Malin took a deep breath, and her eyes filled with tears. "My guy at DHS is dead, Dutch."

"We need to talk to Doc now, Malin."

"We do."

"Where is Ghafor?" I asked when Doc answered my call.

"Not far from here."

"Malin is suggesting you pull Striker."

"I figured that was coming, but my guess is he knows more than she thinks he does."

"What makes you say that?"

"It's a hunch," said Doc, "but he got wind of some stuff going on that didn't sit right with him. That's when he contacted us."

"Rather than pursuing it?"

"That's right."

"Shit," I muttered after ending the call. Whatever the hell Malin had been investigating was big enough to make Striker leave the CIA.

"What did he say?"

"Ghafor is in California."

"And?"

"If you're sure you want to do this, we can leave tomorrow."

"What about Striker?"

"Doc believes that whatever the hell you've uncovered precipitated Striker leaving the CIA. Oh, and Ranger and Diesel are no longer with the agency either. They were given their marching orders when they got back from Somalia."

"They must've been getting close."

"Were they in on it?"

"They were connected."

"To the DHS guy?"

Malin nodded, her eyes filling with tears again.

"Talk to me, baby."

She looked away, wiping at her cheeks.

I put my hands on Malin's shoulders. "I know you're not ready to tell me what your theory is, or how you, Ranger, and Diesel were connected to someone at DHS, but I want you to know that I've got your back no matter what."

"I appreciate it, Dutch. I really do."

"He was important to you," I said, wiping at her tears, trying not to focus on the hurt I felt, knowing that another man meant this much to her, when she was the one in pain over someone she obviously cared deeply for.

"It's...my...fault."

"Whoa, whoa. Don't go there, Malin. If anything, he was the one who put you in danger, not the other way around."

She shook her head, crying harder now.

"Did you ask him to share the information with you?"

"No, but..."

"There isn't any reason for you to take responsibility for his death. None."

At least now it was obvious why she only went so far with what she was willing to tell me, and then abruptly stopped. Malin believed that the guy at DHS died in order to bring what he'd stumbled on to light.

She was protecting me, and I didn't need her to; I wanted to be the one doing the protecting.

Malin went back to looking at something on the computer, and suddenly, her head snapped up.

"Who gave the mission to Striker to go in and get Tackle and Halo out of Somalia?"

"It was an agency job—"

"Exactly. And who was assigned to go along?"

"Word was Ranger and Diesel volunteered."

"Has that been confirmed?"

I didn't know; there wouldn't have been any reason to doubt what Striker's contact at the agency told him. Had they been trying to kill them all with one stone? If so, Mantis and I might very well have been collateral damage if they'd succeeded.

"Tell me about it," Malin asked.

"Striker got the call on Thanksgiving Day," I began. "Several of the K19 partners were at Razor and Gunner's duplex in California."

I'd been there with Alegria. Mantis had been there too, although I hadn't expected him to be, and when we arrived and Mantis saw us, it was clear he'd been kept in the dark too.

"Mantis was the only pilot there, other than Alegria, who wasn't cleared to fly."

"He had no choice," murmured Malin.

"He would've volunteered anyway. That's just who Mantis is."

"How did you get involved?"

"By Christmas, the news wasn't good. Mantis and Striker had both been out of contact long enough that

Doc thought it warranted sending a team in to look for them." I'd been first to volunteer followed by Onyx.

"We found Striker and the other two almost right away, but he and Mantis had separated at one point. My contacts in Mogadishu said there was chatter that another group of Somalis had him."

While Onyx piloted the other three men back to the States, I went after Mantis, found him, and brought him home too.

"The whole thing had been an enormous Charlie Foxtrot, or so it appeared at the time. Now it seems as though it may have been closer to a carefully executed plan."

"I'm sorry, Dutch."

I looked into her eyes. "What for?"

"That I kept looking."

"From the way I see it, Striker and the other two would've been targeted regardless. You had no idea Striker was involved, at least not on the side of the good guys."

Malin still didn't look convinced, but if what she uncovered was as big as it seemed, she was right to question whether there was anyone she could trust.

"Why aren't we leaving until tomorrow?"

I walked closer and put my arm around her shoulders. "First of all, I'm not ready to give up our pretend life yet."

"Dutch—"

"Hang on. The real reason is that we can't get transport until morning, and neither of us is flying commercial with what you've told me so far."

She smiled, which was quickly becoming something that brought me to my knees. Her smile—hell, all of her—was so damn beautiful. She took my breath away.

"We've got about sixteen hours to kill. What do you say? Keep working this or take a break and go back to pretending we're retired and have nothing to do but run and kayak—and, you know—make love?"

"I'm all for pretending, but I need to run, Dutch."

"I know, I know," I grumbled, feeling a lot like the old man she had accused me of being a day or so ago. When had that been? Yesterday? I had no idea what day it was. I sure wished I could go on not needing to.

# 16

*Malin*

I took off ahead of him. I had to. I felt as though my insides were trying to crawl out through my skin; that's how anxiety-ridden I was. If I didn't run, I'd end up having a mental meltdown.

Dutch caught up with me at the same place he had the first day we arrived, although this time he didn't look quite as exhausted.

"I found the shed on my way," he said, holding out a blanket. "Remember, before our kayak ride, how we both agreed that we prefer the other to be naked?"

I smiled and nodded.

"I say we take advantage of what's left of daylight to do just that." When he pulled his shirt over his head and tossed it on the sand, I did too.

"I like this," I said, waiting for him to take off his shorts. Dutch toed off his shoes, bent over to shed his socks, and then walked over to me.

"What about your shorts?"

"Not until I get a chance to look at you." He took my arms that were crossed in front of my breasts, put them at my sides, and then knelt in front of me. "I could get used to this," he said, capturing one of my nipples between his teeth.

I put my hands on his shoulders and dug my nails in as everything he did with his mouth heated me through to my core.

Dutch stood, dropped his shorts on the sand near his other stuff, and led me to the blanket.

He lay down first and eased me on top of him. "Kiss me, Malin. You kiss me."

I put my hands on either side of his face and brought my lips to his. He let me take over; the only thing he did was wrap his arms around my waist.

"I love this," he murmured. "More than you could ever know."

"It was always good between us, wasn't it, Dutch?"

"It was, baby. Damn good. In fact, the best."

Everything in me screamed not to go back to asking him why, then, he chose another woman over me. He'd already told me how he felt and how he knew he didn't love Alegria the way he once thought he had. The time had come for me to let it go. He'd told me he was sorry, multiple times.

I pulled back and looked into his eyes. "I have to tell you something." I bit my bottom lip, and Dutch tightened his grip.

"Go ahead."

"I forgive you."

He brought his hands up to my face and held me still, even when I tried to bring my lips back to his.

"Are you sure?"

"Yes."

"It can't be about anything else, Malin."

"What do you mean?"

"This is between me and you. What I did."

"That's all it is, Dutch. But there's more."

When he let go of me, I stood, walked over, and grabbed my shirt.

Dutch sat up and put his elbows on his knees. "Whatever you have to say to me you can say without your shirt on."

"I don't think I can." If I was going to be as big a person as Dutch was, I had to stick to my resolve and apologize for what I did.

He stayed right where he was, not even attempting to grab his shorts.

"You're kind of distracting that way."

"Which way is that?"

"Naked."

"I'm fine unless I'm making you uncomfortable."

"This might be easier if you put your shorts on." I picked them up and tossed them his way.

He stood and pulled them up over his hips. "Better?"

"Yes, thank you."

"Tell me whatever it is, Malin."

"We need to talk about Germany."

"Ah," he said, nodding his head.

"I knew you were stopping at Ramstein for a meeting with AIRCOM before going on to Somalia to meet with Mohamed Abdullahi and with Ahmed Umar."

# 17

*Dutch*

I looked down at the sand and rolled my shoulders. My meeting at the headquarters of both the United States Air Force in Europe and also for NATO Allied Air Command was supposed to be known only to those directly involved—with top-level security clearance. Malin had the clearance, but there was no reason she should have been read in on that meeting.

"You came looking for me?"

"I made the arrangements for the pickup."

"I see." Shortly after I arrived in Germany, I'd been waiting for transport when the last thing I remembered was being hit over the head.

"It was the only way I could get to Ghafor."

"By delivering me to Zamed Safi?"

The man with connections to al-Qaeda and his goons had beaten me close to death and caused my temporary amnesia. I'd escaped only to be found wandering the streets of Germany by Malin, and set up a second time for capture. Safi hadn't really wanted me; he'd wanted

Mantis, who had been responsible for the death of both of Safi's brothers. I was the bait to lure Mantis there.

"I'm sorry, Dutch."

I got up and walked over to the water.

"Tell me why you did it."

"I told you it was the only way I could get access to Ghafor. I had to prove myself."

"You're sure?"

"That's all it was, Dutch."

"I want to know the truth, Malin."

"If you're suggesting I did it out of some kind of revenge, I resent the accusation."

"I had to ask."

"That wasn't what it was, Dutch, and again, I'm sorry," she said. "At the time, I asked myself what you would do."

I turned around. "And?"

"I knew you'd keep the mission going."

"Like I did in Islamabad?"

Malin scrunched her eyes. "That wasn't your mission."

"If it had been, do you think I would've let Orlov kill you just to keep it going? If you do, you don't know me at all." I picked up my shirt, socks, and shoes. "I'll catch up with you later."

"Wait!" she shouted after me, but I ignored her. I needed time to think not only about the fact that she'd set me up, which I'd already known, but that she believed it's what I would've done too.

Instead of taking the most direct trail up to the house, I kept going along the shoreline, stopping when it rounded a bend, to put on my socks and shoes.

There was an unspoken deal among the K19 partners. If the life of someone we cared about was threatened, the objective of an op immediately changed to rescue and/or extraction. No questions asked.

When the rest of the team and I had gone in to get Alegria after she was kidnapped and held for a hundred-million-dollar ransom, we were given direct orders from the CIA not to jeopardize Malin's op.

I'd ignored those orders, shot, and killed the man who held Malin with a gun to her head, and blew her mission.

"Doc, I have a question for you," I said when the man answered my call.

"Shoot."

"When Alegria was kidnapped at the hotel in Islamabad, her father reported that an American woman had been involved. We've determined that Kilbourne was that woman, right?"

"That's right. Tell me why you're confirming that at this particular time. It's old news, Dutch."

"Malin just confessed that she set me up in Ramstein. She was behind the initial abduction."

"That's really not a surprise," Doc said after a heavy sigh. "Again, why are we talking about this now?"

"She set me up first, and then Alegria. You add them together, and you get revenge."

"Let me ask you the only question that matters."

"Go ahead."

"Do you believe that's who Malin is?"

There was one person who could give me an account of the other things Malin had done—Alegria. However, I couldn't talk to her now. It would be too risky. The fewer people who knew what Malin was caught up in, the better, at least until we could find out how bad it really was.

# 18

*Malin*

I watched Dutch walk away, knowing three things. First, he may never forgive me for what I'd done. Second, I hadn't had any choice. If we had any chance at all at having a relationship, we couldn't go into it without honesty on both our parts. And finally, the worst part was, I wasn't finished.

There was another thing I'd done that I needed him to know. As a condition of Ghafor giving me the information I needed about where the money had come from and why it had been paid out to him, I was forced to arrange and execute the kidnapping of Alegria Mondreau.

That alone, though, hadn't been enough for the leader of the Islamic State. He'd also demanded that I be the one to hold the K19 pilot hostage until his demand of a ransom in the amount of a hundred million dollars was paid.

At the time, I thought the amount was ludicrous and told him it would never happen, but Ghafor knew something I hadn't. Alegria's father was a billionaire.

That Ghafor was with Striker now, told me that he was likely trying to negotiate the exchange of the same information I'd been waiting for, but had never gotten.

There were two reasons why I prayed Striker hadn't been able to convince Ghafor to give it to him. First, if the former agent was on the inside of the whole conspiracy, he'd know everything I knew and more, essentially signing my death warrant.

If Striker wasn't on the inside, once he knew everything I did, it would be his own death warrant he'd be signing.

On top of that, there was one more significant bit of information I didn't have, and it hadn't been coming from Ghafor. It had been up to Orlov to determine whether United Russia was behind the money coming into the US in the first place. Dutch had killed him before I had a chance to find out.

If that was the case, it would be impossible for me to prove now. I shuddered to think what it would mean if UR had been. The ramifications were widespread enough that it could threaten democracy in a way that may be irrevocable.

I sat on the sand and looked out at the water. The mission I'd undertaken was the most important of my life, but not my career. In fact, it was a career-killer.

Right or wrong, I'd risked everything in order to complete the mission. If I was ever able to get my hands on those last two pieces of information and what I'd uncovered came to light, there would be ramifications as far-reaching as the White House.

"Hi," I said when Dutch walked in the back door of the house and found me sitting at the kitchen counter.

"Hi." He walked over and stood in front of me.

"Dutch, I—"

"Before you say anything, we need to talk about Alegria."

"That's exactly what I was going to say."

"Go ahead." He sat on the stool next to me.

Dutch listened as I explained that Ghafor had made my involvement in Alegria's kidnapping a condition of turning over the information I needed.

"I wouldn't have let him kill her," I added. "There's one more thing you should know."

Dutch looked into my eyes.

"I knew that Zamed was taking you to Islamabad. I also knew the location where he planned to keep you."

"That's how Doc and Razor found me as quickly as they did."

"That's right."

"But they didn't know the information came through you."

"They didn't, but if you doubt what I'm telling you is true, I can prove it."

Dutch leaned forward, at first putting his elbows on his knees, but he didn't stop there; he rested his head on my lap.

When I ran my fingers through his hair, Dutch sat up and took my hands in his.

"I don't need you to prove anything to me."

"Dutch...do you...can you ever..."

"If I had stayed and we had talked this out, we could have continued our pretend life here on the island a lot earlier." He rolled his shoulders. "I'm not sure I can say I forgive you, if that's what you're looking for."

"Okay..."

"Is what you did something you should be forgiven for, or did you do what you had to do while, at the same time, ensuring the least amount of collateral damage? At great risk to yourself, I might add."

"That's what I meant earlier. When I said that I asked myself what you would do. I knew that no matter what, you'd make sure whoever you put in danger would be rescued as soon as possible."

"Are you also the one who gave us the intel about where Alegria was being held?"

I nodded and bit my bottom lip. "Why did you walk away and leave me at the shore earlier?"

"I had to process through whether what you did was out of revenge. I'm sorry, Malin, but I needed time to think."

"What made you come back to the house now?"

"I realized something about both of us."

I waited for him to continue.

"There is one person who could tell me about how things went down in Islamabad. That person is Alegria. However, I knew I couldn't contact her and ask her, because more than I needed to know what she'd tell me, I needed to protect you. That's when I knew you'd done the things you had because you had no other choice, not to put Alegria and me in danger."

"It's the truth, Dutch."

"It's also why you won't tell me your theory. You don't want me to be in the same kind of danger you are. Montgomery warned you away from the money trail. When we arrived back in the States, you believed the agency was going to burn you. Both of those things tell me that the CIA is involved."

"Yes," I whispered.

"How far-reaching is it, Malin?"

"All the way to the top."

"To the president?"

"Yes," I whispered again.

"Is it something they'd kill you over?"

I didn't respond, but he was smart enough to answer his own question.

"Thank you for trusting me enough to tell me."

"How did you know?"

"That you were into something this deep?"

"Yes."

"I told you—intuition, instinct, my gut. Whatever you want to call it. The way you looked at me when Orlov had his gun to your head. I thought it was him that you were afraid of. You told me that he wouldn't have killed you, and now I believe you. You weren't afraid of him; you were afraid of me."

"More that the mission was ending before I had the final pieces to ensure my safety. Not that if I had anything, it would've been enough."

"What was Sergei's role?"

"Finding out if United Russia was involved and if so, how."

"I killed him before he could brief you."

"That's right."

"What does your gut tell you?"

"He wouldn't have shown up if they weren't."

"Exactly. Now we have to figure out how. What's your theory?"

"That the money came from them in the first place."

"What about Ghafor? What piece of information were you waiting for from him?"

"What he did to earn the money."

"We'll meet Onyx at the dock in the morning. He'll fly us to California, and by tomorrow afternoon, maybe we'll have some answers."

"Striker may have them already."

Dutch nodded. "If I were in your position, I wouldn't be convinced I could trust Striker either, or Ranger or Diesel. Let's do an inventory of who you feel you can trust at this point. I want you to be completely honest with me about it too, Malin. If there's anyone you are unsure of, they need to go on a different list."

"You."

Dutch smiled. "Is that it?"

"No. Onyx."

"What about Sofia?"

"I don't have any reason not to."

"What about Doc?"

I shrugged. "You seem to trust him."

"With my life, but this isn't my list. If you're unsure, he goes on the third list."

"People I trust, those I don't, and ones I'm unsure of."

"That's right."

"Most everyone is on the unsure list. Striker, though, I'd add to the list of people I don't trust."

"Roger that."

"You aren't going to try to convince me otherwise?"

"Absolutely not."

He checked his phone. "Nothing yet."

"Let me guess, you're hungry."

Dutch laughed out loud. "It's never a question of whether I am or not, just to what degree."

"Are you getting tired of Spanish food yet?"

"No…"

I stood and walked over to the pantry and then opened the refrigerator.

"You're in luck."

"Yeah?"

"Yep. Although you'll have to accept marinara from a jar." I pulled ground beef and eggs out of the fridge, then pasta, sauce, and breadcrumbs from the cupboard.

"You have no idea how happy I am right now. Anything I can do to help?"

"Would you mind seeing if we can piece together garlic bread?"

"In exchange for your spaghetti and meatballs? It's the least I'd be willing to do."

"Well, you did save my life."

"I did, Malin."

"Thank you," I murmured. "It means a lot that you have my back, Dutch."

He walked over and put his arm around my shoulders, pulled me close, and kissed my forehead. "Always, baby. I hope you know how sincerely I mean that."

Dutch devoured three-quarters of the pound of spaghetti I cooked, and all but two of the meatballs.

"You can have the last one."

"Are you sure?"

I laughed. "Do you really like them that much, or do you just pretend to make me feel good?"

Dutch leaned forward, grabbed my neck, and pulled me so our foreheads touched. "I don't like them; I love them."

I studied his mouth as he spoke, yearning to feel his lips on mine.

"A half hour ago, I wouldn't have done this, but now I can't stop myself."

He kissed me, pushing his tongue through my lips. "I'll clean up later," he said, standing and taking my hand.

I followed him up the two flights to the bedroom, already trembling with want.

"I can't get enough of you." He pulled my shirt over my head.

"Me either," I said, doing the same with his.

Once we were both naked, we lay on the bed and stretched out on our sides, facing one another.

Dutch took his time, moving his eyes over my body. Our languid lovemaking was at once pleasure-filled and painfully slow, but I wouldn't want him to do anything differently.

There was a connection between us that had nothing to do with frenzy. It was sensuous and unhurried, so full of love that I thought my heart would burst.

The way Dutch looked at me filled my heart—it was as though I was the sexiest, most precious, most loved woman alive.

He held me so tight, so close to him, like he'd never let me go. His fingers dug into my flesh, and when I thought our bodies couldn't get any closer, he tightened his grip until as much of our skin as possible was flush against the other's.

Soon we'd have to leave our pretend life and go out and face the uncertainty of my real one.

I'd gone it alone for so long that it was hard to let myself lean on Dutch, but knowing he'd be with me when we left the island, eased my worry.

"What are you thinking so hard about, baby?"

I smiled down at him. "Not wanting to leave even though I know I have no choice."

Dutch sat up. "You do have a choice. We can stay right here and let the K19 team on the West Coast sort this out with Ghafor."

I shook my head. "I can't. I started this mission, and I have to see it through."

# 19

*Dutch*

An unfamiliar feeling took hold of my chest and wouldn't let go. My eyes lingered on Malin's body—her gorgeous, delectable, mind-blowingly sexy body, and I found myself looking deeper. I stared into her eyes flecked with brown, green, and blue, that changed so often, and felt as though I could see the purity of Malin's soul.

Was I confusing my need to protect her, take care of her, keep her safe, with loving her? Or did I feel all of those things *because* I loved her?

I could no longer go so slow. Passion overtook me as I moved over her again. "I need you now, baby."

When her body arched and yielded to mine, I came so close to saying the words I vowed I never would because I'd convinced myself I'd never feel them.

Did I love Malin Kilbourne? As more than someone I was protecting? Did I love her as the woman I wanted to spend my life with? I didn't know. Not yet anyway.

"Dutch," she groaned.

"Shh," I whispered. "Just let me love you, Malin."

"Doc said to come straight to the house in Montecito after we land," Onyx told me the next day when Malin and I boarded the plane.

"Who's flying with you?"

"Corazón."

"Where is she?"

Onyx motioned toward the back of the plane, where I saw her talking to Malin.

"How'd things go the rest of the time on the island?" he asked.

"It got worse before it got better, and then it got great."

"Glad to hear it, bro."

I rolled my eyes and walked back to join the two women.

"I'll talk more with you later," I heard Sofia say to Malin before she walked past me.

"You two seem to get along well."

"She's very nice."

"So are you."

Malin smiled. "Thank you, Dutch. You're pretty nice too."

I took her hand in mine after we'd chosen seats and fastened our seat belts.

"How are you doing?"

"Okay. Better than I would be if you weren't with me."

I put my hand on my heart. "That's about the nicest thing you've ever said to me."

When Malin put her arm through mine and rested her head on my shoulder, I felt ten feet taller than I was. Malin was the most independent woman I'd ever known, even more so than Alegria. Having her put her trust in me filled me with pride.

"I'm so tired."

I reclined my seat and hers, and she rested her head on my shoulder.

I kissed her forehead. "Sleep, baby."

# 20

*Malin*

"Wow," I gasped when we drove up to the gates of Doc and Merrigan's Montecito compound.

"I know. It's impressive," said Dutch.

"It's so beautiful," Sofia said from the front seat of the SUV, glancing over at Onyx, who was driving.

"It's definitely my dream house," said Onyx.

The outside of the Spanish Colonial Revival house was white stucco with dark-brown shutters and a red-tile roof. Balconies with wrought-iron railings extended from every upstairs room, and massive palm trees, which looked old enough to have been planted before the house was built, stretched high above the roofline. Bright-pink bougainvillea grew up the side walls of the five-car garage near where Onyx parked the SUV that had been waiting for us at the airfield. Weathered terra-cotta pots, overflowing with flowers and vines, dotted the circular drive and the welcoming entryway leading to the massive wooden door.

"Welcome." Doc walked out holding a baby. "This is Laird," he said when the boy tried to squirm out of his arms.

"How old is he?" I asked, holding out my finger for him to grab.

"Almost five months."

"Big for his age?" I asked.

"Gigantic. Come on, Merrigan is inside." Doc motioned toward the door that led into the main room. It had massive dark wood beams on the ceiling and a fireplace that sat opposite the front door and matched the color of the home's exterior.

Dark leather chairs and sofas sat on the tile floors and Mexican rugs. We walked from that room into the kitchen, the dining room, and out a double door that led to a patio where Merrigan was snipping herbs from a large pot similar to the ones that lined the driveway and front door.

"Hi," she said, setting her shears and the herbs on the table and wiping her hands on her pants. "You must be Malin," she said with an accent that sounded more Scottish than English.

"It's nice to meet you." I shook the woman's outstretched hand. "You have a beautiful home, and baby."

"I have to admit that I think so too, although I'm not sure how long we'll be able to call Laird beautiful." Merrigan smiled at her husband, who beamed back at her. "He's handsome, right, Kade?"

The woman hugged Dutch and Onyx and then introduced herself to Sofia.

"He wants his mum," Merrigan said when the baby scrambled from his father's arms to hers. "Are you hungry?" she asked.

"How about you, Dutch? Are you hungry?" I smiled.

Dutch grabbed my neck, pulled me close to him, and kissed my temple. "You're teasing me."

I put my arm around his waist and my head on his shoulder. "He's always hungry."

"Lunch is almost ready," Merrigan told us, leading us back into the house.

"Can I help?" I asked when she set the baby in a high chair and started pulling things out of the refrigerator. "Although I won't be as helpful as Sofia, given she's a veritable chef."

Merrigan clapped her hands and directed Sofia to where she had several ingredients ready for a large salad.

"You could slice the bread, if you wouldn't mind."

I turned the warm loaf upside down before slicing it.

"You're a baker," Merrigan commented.

"Not as much as I used to be, but my dad and I always made fresh bread on the weekend."

"That's a lovely memory."

I murmured in agreement and looked over at Dutch, who was studying me. Heat spread down my neck when he winked at me.

"Is it a bad thing to say I love seeing her in the kitchen?" I heard Dutch ask Doc and Onyx, who were sitting with him at the table.

"I don't know. Is it, Fatale?" Doc asked his wife.

"It doesn't bother me. Does it you, Malin? What about you, Sofia?"

"My dream is to own a restaurant," Sofia responded, turning to look at Onyx, who was beaming at her in the same way Dutch was looking at me and Doc at Merrigan.

"Malin?" Dutch asked.

"It doesn't bother me," I said, sneaking another glance at the man who was looking at me like I would be as good to eat as the lunch we were preparing. "Sometimes it's nice to be normal."

I had no doubt Merrigan knew exactly what I meant. Until recently, the woman had been a high-ranking MI6 agent and, from what I'd heard, was now the managing partner of K19 Security Solutions.

Merrigan smiled and handed me a bowl of salad that I set on the table.

"She makes me eat salad first," Doc told both men.

"Don't worry, I have panini ready to go under the press, and there's pie fresh out of the oven."

While Sofia, Merrigan, and I cleaned up from lunch, Doc motioned Dutch and Onyx out of the room. A feeling of dread settled in the pit of my stomach. Something was up; I could sense it.

"Oh, dear," said Merrigan, obviously picking up on the same thing I had.

When Dutch came back into the kitchen, I turned to face him, drying my hands on a towel. "What's happened?"

"We don't know all the details yet, but there's been an ambush."

Merrigan dropped the dish she had been drying, and it shattered on the tile floor. "Sorry," she said, bending to pick up the pieces.

"I'll get it in a minute," Doc said, holding out his hand for her to stand.

"Tell us, Kade," Merrigan said to her husband.

When he looked over and said, "Ghafor is dead," I felt my knees go weak and grabbed the counter. Suddenly, Dutch was by my side.

"What about the team?" Merrigan asked.

"Striker has been transported via medical helicopter. They're driving Ranger by ambulance. Monk and Diesel were able to take down the two shooters."

"Who are they?" I asked.

"They haven't been identified yet."

"What is Striker's condition?" Merrigan asked.

"He's in surgery now," answered Doc.

When Dutch touched my arm, I turned and let him take me into his arms.

The ramifications of what Ghafor's death meant raced through my mind. Who had killed him? More importantly, how had they found him? Wouldn't K19 have held him in the securest of locations? If four operatives couldn't keep him safe, what did that mean for me? My biggest question, though, was whether Striker had been able to get Ghafor to talk, and if so, was it enough for me to be able to prove at least part of the conspiracy I'd uncovered?

"We'll transport the four of you to the airfield." Doc looked directly at Dutch and Onyx.

"I'm leaving?"

"Until we know who the shooters were and get a handle on how they located our team, yes. You are leaving."

"No. I need to know what Striker knows before I go anywhere."

Dutch looked at me. "Malin…"

"Kade." Merrigan put her hand on her husband's arm. "This is her mission to complete."

"What about the safe house in Harmony?" asked Dutch.

"You'll be safer at the ranch," Doc answered, turning to Dutch and then to me. "It's less than two hours from here. We'll keep you briefed on what we learn in real time."

I looked at Merrigan, who nodded.

"Appreciate this, Doc," said Dutch.

"What is the ranch?" I asked.

"Butler Ranch. It's my family's place outside of Paso Robles. There are few locations on the Central Coast of California, outside of Vandenberg Air Force Base, as secure as my father keeps that place."

"Doc's father is Burns Butler. Have you heard of him?" Merrigan asked.

"Of course." Everyone in my line of work knew of Laird "Burns" Butler. He was a legend in the intelligence world, just like his son was.

"Transport?" Dutch asked.

Doc looked at Onyx. "I'd prefer air."

"Roger that," he answered, pulling his phone out of his pocket. "'Copter?"

Doc nodded, taking a fussy Laird out of the high chair. "Nap time, big boy," he said, carrying him out of the room.

"Come with me." Merrigan led me out of the room. "You too," she added, looking at Sofia before walking out to the patio.

"The ranch is beautiful and secure, as Kade said. Laird and Sorcha live there full-time along with Naughton and his wife, Bradley. There's a cottage no one lives in presently and an apartment above the winery."

"Winery?" I asked.

"There's vineyard and winery along with a working ranch. You'll be safe there, and also as Kade said, it isn't that far from here, and there's a helipad."

I raised a brow.

"Two of my brothers-in-law, including the one who still lives on the ranch, are helicopter pilots."

"Wow," I murmured. "Doc's family is…"

"Bigger than life?" Merrigan smiled. "You don't know the half of it." She studied me for a minute. "You and Sorcha, Kade's mum, will get on quite well," she added. "She'll adore you. You, too, Sofia."

"Ready?" Dutch asked when he found us still out on the patio.

"Yes," I said, but held back a moment after Sofia thanked Merrigan and went back into the house.

Merrigan took both of my hands in hers. "I'll make sure that everything we know, you do too. I won't let my husband or anyone else on the K19 team hold anything back from you."

"I appreciate it, the mission…"

"It's more than the mission. It's your life."

Merrigan's eyes met Dutch's, and he nodded, motioning for us to follow him back inside.

"Reports are that Striker is out of surgery. He's stable," said Doc.

"And Ranger?" I asked.

"He's stable too, but otherwise, I don't know anything about his condition. As information comes in to us, we'll make sure you're briefed." Doc looked at a message on his phone.

"What now?" Dutch asked.

"McTiernan responded to my request for a meeting."

My grip on Dutch's hand tightened.

"If I find out he had anything to do with the attempted murder of two K19 partners along with two other men contracted with our firm, I'll rip both of the little weasel's arms off," Doc added.

Dutch put his arm around my shoulders. "Let's go," he said, kissing my temple.

# 21

*Dutch*

Onyx flew north along the coastline from Santa Barbara past Morro Rock and then turned inland.

"It's breathtaking," Malin said through the mic on the headset.

I'd always loved the Central Coast with its rocky shores along the Pacific Ocean combined with the Redwoods and Monterey Pines that Big Sur, only a couple of hours north, was so well known for.

Moments after the helicopter went east, rows and rows of vineyard after vineyard covered the land beneath us.

If I were to compare it to Cokabow Island off South Carolina's coast, though, its beauty wouldn't measure up. Whenever I closed my eyes and imagined the shoreline, I saw the one thing that made it utterly unique—Malin's naked body resting on mine as we lay on the sand.

The pretend life we'd lived there, even for only a handful of days, had become my ideal. When this was all over, when Malin was safe, I'd make her the offer of buying the island for the second time, knowing even now that the only way I'd do it is if she would agree to live there with me.

"What are you thinking about?" she asked through the mic.

I smiled. "Cokabow."

Malin squeezed my hand. "Me too."

How different this was from our first helicopter flight when she'd refused to look at or speak to me unless it was combatively. I brought our woven hands to my mouth and kissed the back of hers. The smile she gave me in return made my heart swell.

Onyx landed the helicopter, and we waited for the blades to stop their rotation. By the time we climbed out, Burns and Sorcha were standing outside of the helipad's circle, waiting for us.

After introductions were made, Sorcha asked if anyone was hungry. I was, like always, but when no one else said they were, I kept quiet. Malin tugged my arm, which made me smile.

"How about a tour?" suggested Sorcha.

As many times as I'd been here, there were still things I didn't notice before about the ranch and the vineyards.

"Have you been in the caves?" Sorcha asked me.

"I haven't."

"You're in for a treat," said Burns, unlocking the gate and leading us inside.

The temperature outside was in the low sixties. Once we got a few feet inside the cave's entrance, it dropped at least twenty degrees. I put my arm around Malin and drew her body closer to me.

As we went deeper into the cave, Burns and Sorcha pointed out the various rooms used for wine barrel storage. Eventually we came to a large open space set up as a tasting area. Wine racks held hundreds of bottles on all four sides of the room, and were even built in above the archways that opened to offshoots on every side.

"How much more is there?" Malin asked.

"Oh, lass," answered Sorcha. "Miles and miles at times it seems."

"Care for a taste?" asked Burns, pulling the plug out of a bunghole in a barrel that sat under the racks of wine.

"Would love it," I answered.

"This is Bradley's," he said, pulling wine from the barrel through a long glass tube called a thief.

"Bradley is our daughter-in-law," explained Sorcha. "Other than my Maddox, she is the best winemaker in all of California."

"Some might argue that she's even better than he is," said a man coming in from the direction we had.

"I'm Naughton," he said, introducing himself to Malin and Sofia. "Good to see you guys," he added, shaking my hand and then Onyx's.

"Naughton manages all of the vineyards both here and at the Demetria Estate, which belongs to Maddox, one of our other sons as you may have gathered from Sorcha's comment," said Burns.

Naughton took the thief from his father's hand and put it back in the barrel, pulling out more wine.

"We'll see after the harvest, but I'd be willing to bet that Bradley's Butler Ranch Highland Zin takes gold and Maddox's Demetria takes silver."

After sampling from three other barrels, Laird led us back out to the cave's entrance. I was already outside when I realized Malin wasn't right behind me. I turned and saw her hugging Sorcha while Burns looked on.

"What do you think of this place?" I asked Malin a few minutes later as we followed our hosts and the rest of the group, walking the rolling hills.

"It's incredible."

"Better than Cokabow?"

"Nothing could be better than our island," she answered, winking.

"Mmm, I like the sound of that." I pulled her into my arms, holding her back to allow the others to go on without us.

"We're going to the winery," I shouted when Burns turned back in our direction. The man waved behind him.

"We are?"

"We haven't had a chance to talk, alone."

"We need to?"

I pulled her over to a boulder that sat near one of the sloping vineyards, picked her up, and set her on it. I stood between her legs, putting my hands on either side of her hips.

"Talk to me, baby. Tell me what you're thinking."

"Mostly about whether Striker got Ghafor to talk, and how much he knows. If anything."

"What about McTiernan?"

"I don't know what to think. Like Striker, it's hard to know which side he's on."

"If the agency is involved in the ambush, then they've upped their ante considerably."

"It's unlikely we'll be able to connect the two dead guys to them," she said unnecessarily.

"No, but attempted murder of four former agents will be looked into by Homeland Security. "Sorry," I said when I saw her flinch.

"Burns wants to meet with me."

"Is that a conversation you want to have on your own?"

# 22

*Malin*

Did I? I didn't think Dutch would make such an offer, considering he was in full-on bodyguard mode. Given the choice, though, I'd rather have him by my side than not. "No."

Dutch let out the breath I hadn't noticed he was holding.

"There will come a time you're going to have to let me out of your sight, Dutch," I teased, but by the look on his face, he didn't think it was funny.

"Why?" he asked, moving closer. "Why do you have to be out of my sight, Malin?"

"Because...our lives...we have separate lives, Dutch."

"What if I don't want to have separate lives?"

I wasn't sure what to say. The circumstances that forced us to be together wouldn't exist forever, and I wouldn't want them to. The sooner I could extricate myself from whatever dirty deeds the CIA had done, the better.

Once it was over, and I prayed it would be over, I didn't know what would happen between Dutch and me. He would still be a K19 partner, and I had no idea what I'd want to do. The only thing I'd ever considered doing once I retired was applying for a professorship at the University of Virginia—my alma mater.

I looked up at the pained expression on Dutch's face.

"It's taking you too long to respond," he said.

"I don't know, to be honest."

"Fair enough."

"Just like that?"

"For now." He grabbed my hand and pulled me in the direction of the house. "Let's go see what we can find to eat."

When we got close to the cottages, I saw someone waving at us from the porch of the main house.

"Hi," said the woman, walking out to meet them with a baby in her arms.

"Lots of babies in this family," mumbled Dutch.

"I'm Bradley," she said when we got closer. "And this is Charlie, who appears to have gotten in a fight with his lunch." She tried to wipe the red sauce stains off his shirt, which made the baby giggle.

After I introduced myself and Dutch, we followed her back up the porch steps and through the door.

"It's hard to imagine I was once a professional wine-maker, organized, cleanly." She laughed, picking up toys as she made her way into the house.

"We tasted some of your wine earlier," I told her. "It was very good."

"Oh. Thanks." She put the baby down on the floor with a pile of toys and plopped down in one of the chairs. "He's getting so heavy." She motioned for us to have a seat as well, and as soon as we had, she jumped back up.

"Sorcha sent me a message saying she thought you might be hungry. I'm sorry to say there is no pasta left. I could make a quick sandwich if you'd like."

"I can make it," said Dutch, standing and walking toward the kitchen. "You sit back down."

"He's one of those," giggled Bradley once Dutch was out of the room.

"Those?"

"All of Kade's partners are so alpha, aren't they? I mean it isn't just his partners; his brothers are all the same way."

"There's my Charlie," squealed Sorcha, walking in the front door with Burns and Naughton in tow.

"Onyx is taking Sofia back to the airport," said Burns. "She said she'd be in touch."

Moments later, we heard the whir of the helicopter's blades.

"Is he coming back?" I asked.

"Straightaway," he answered. "Would you like me to show you where you'll be staying?"

"Um, yes, please. Dutch is just making a sandwich."

Burns smiled. "We'll wait. I'd rather not wind up on Miller's bad side for whisking you away."

"I'm here." Dutch came out carrying two sandwiches.

"You'll stay in the cottage that used to be Maddox's." Burns motioned to the various structures once we were outside. "Onyx will stay in the apartment."

"Is that the winery?" I asked, pointing to a building that looked as though it had once been a barn.

"And tasting room, although we are no longer open to the public for tasting here at the vineyard unless it's a special event. Our two daughters-in-law operate a tasting room in Cambria, the little village due west of here, right by the ocean."

"How did you get involved in the business?" I asked.

"I promised Sorcha that we'd retire to the ranch and that we'd raise our family here. My father was the one who started growing grapes, and my mother made wine."

"It seems like a very nice life."

"It is," said Burns, opening the door to a stone cottage.

My bags and Dutch's were already in the entryway.

"After you." Burns led us into the living room.

Dutch went into the kitchen with his sandwiches and came back empty-handed.

"You can eat," I told him.

"I already had one. Those two are for later."

"I'll let you get some rest," said Burns. "I'm sure you've had a very long day."

"You mentioned earlier that you wanted to have a conversation with me."

Burns waved as he went out the front door. "Plenty of time for that tomorrow. Sleep well."

I plopped in a chair similarly to the way Bradley had earlier.

"You're exhausted," said Dutch, pulling me up and over to the couch to sit beside him. "Do you want something to eat before we head upstairs?"

"I'm not that hungry." I rested my head on his shoulder. "I really hoped that I'd have the chance to talk to him tonight."

"I know it's hard to wait, but my intuition is telling me you're close, Malin."

"Every time I feel like I am, something derails me."

Dutch stroked my hair. "I heard a rumor that this cottage has the most spectacular bathroom setup in all of California."

"All of California?"

Dutch stood and pulled me with him. "Let's go see."

"Did Doc say when he and McTiernan were meeting?"

"I don't think he knew yet."

I stopped at the bottom of the stairs. "Can we check?"

Dutch put his arm around my waist. "You don't have to ask my permission nor do you have to ask me to do it for you."

"I know. I just..." I rested my forehead on his chest. "God, who am I?"

"You're dead tired. Let's check in with Doc and then get some rest."

"There is one other thing preventing me from contacting Doc myself."

"What's that?"

"I don't have a phone, Dutch."

I watched Dutch send the text. As he'd said, I was dead tired, not just from today or the last week, but more from the last several months. There were many times over the course of a mission, when things turned into more of an investigation, that I questioned why I didn't just let it go.

I thought a lot about what my father would tell me to do if he were still alive. There had even been times when I'd wondered what Dutch would say.

When Dutch's phone vibrated, he held it out for me to see.

*McTiernan to arrive in the morning. Will brief you after our meeting.*

Dutch walked into the bathroom and tried to figure out how to use the control panel that was on a wall between a large open shower and a tub big enough for the two of us to sit side by side.

Once he'd filled the tub, he held out his hand to me. I eased into its warmth, but he didn't join me.

"Look what I found," he said, walking over to a mini fridge and holding up a bottle of sparkling wine and two glasses.

"Join me?" I asked, holding my hand out to him.

"I would love to."

Dutch poured two glasses and set them on the edge of the tub. I scooted over to give him room to sit beside me. Once he had, he put one arm around me and handed me a glass with the other.

"Mmm."

"Good?"

"The wine? Yes, it's good, but everything else is great. I really needed this, Dutch."

He ran his finger from my ear, down my neck, to my shoulder.

"You're so brave."

"I'm not."

"You are, and it makes me wish I had the power to carry your anxiety for you. I am in awe of you."

"I remember the first day I met you. I'm not sure if I would call it awe or out-and-out intimidation, but even in those first few minutes, I knew that you were someone I wanted to get to know better."

"I felt the same way."

I turned my head. "You did?"

"Yes, Malin, I did. Every day that you worked for me was absolute torture because I knew that, as long as you did, I couldn't touch you...and I really wanted to touch you."

"I have to admit, I did a lot of daydreaming..."

Dutch smiled. "In meetings."

I laughed. "You knew? Oh, God. Did everyone know?"

"No one else seemed to notice." Dutch set his glass down and then touched a spot on my neck. "Your skin, right here, would flush. That's how I knew." He bent his head and touched the spot with his lips. "And that's what I imagined doing whenever I saw it."

"I'm so embarrassed."

"Why?"

"That instead of thinking about the meeting's agenda, I was thinking about you."

"I couldn't leave the agency fast enough once you started working there. That year was absolute torture."

"I had no idea."

"Even after that first night? I didn't waste any time getting my hands on you."

I felt my skin heat.

"You are so fucking sexy." Dutch took the empty glass from my trembling hand and set it and his out of the way. He put his hands on my waist, lifted me out of the water, and turned me around.

"This is where I want you," he said, easing me back down so I straddled him.

Every time I felt the anxiety over Ghafor and Striker and the mission coming to the front of my mind, I pushed it back.

Dutch soothed me, first with the bath, and then the wine, and then with his body—over and over again. He chased the monsters and dragons away, like my father had, but in his very unique way.

When he told me he'd be right back and left the bedroom, I knew he was headed to the kitchen to get the sandwiches he'd made earlier. The man's appetites, not just for food, were insatiable.

He came back with two plates, handing one to me before climbing back into bed. Before I'd eaten half of the sandwich he gave me, he was done with all of his.

"Here," I said, handing him my plate. "You can finish it."

"Are you sure?"

"I don't think I'll ever be able to eat a quarter of what you do in a day, and yet, look at you. You have zero percent body fat, don't you?"

"I don't pay that much attention, although, you kicked my butt in South Carolina. That worried me a little."

I closed my eyes, imagining again that this was our life. It felt so good to be with him. How quickly would this come to an end once I wrapped my mission, one way or another?

There was a possibility I'd have to walk away without proving anything, and if that was the case, how long would it be before the agency sent someone to ensure I'd never have the opportunity to pursue it again?

It would mean living my life on the run, always looking over my shoulder, never able to relax for fear that each day I woke up, might be my last.

It wasn't a life I could share with anyone. As much as I might be tempted to, I couldn't allow Dutch to live that way.

"Whatever you're thinking about, stop." Dutch reached over and turned off the light on the bedside table and then pulled me close to him. "Sleep, baby."

I doubted I'd be able to, but within minutes, my eyes grew heavy and I fell asleep.

# 23

*Dutch*

When I opened my eyes and saw it was daylight, I eased my arm out from under Malin and slid out of bed. Making my way downstairs, I called Doc.

"How's Striker?" I asked when he answered and said good morning.

"He demanded to see McTiernan last night."

"Is he here already?"

"No. He arrives at ten hundred."

"Any idea who the shooters were?"

"No information yet." Nothing Doc had said surprised me.

"Has Striker given any indication that he was able to get Ghafor to talk?"

"He's insisting that he talk to Malin before he tells anyone else anything."

"He must have something to tell her, then."

"He must."

"But he won't tell you."

"He's always been a damn control freak."

"Are you still convinced he wasn't on the inside of whatever this is?"

Doc murmured his affirmation. "Merrigan shares my opinion."

I remembered hearing that Striker and Doc's wife had once been linked romantically, not that I'd bring it up now—or ever.

"Malin and I can leave to head down there within the next hour."

"Hold off. I want to talk with McTiernan first."

"Roger that."

I went back upstairs; Malin was still asleep, and I had no intention of waking her. She needed rest more than anything, and since Doc didn't want us to come south for another three hours at least, I had no reason not to let her sleep.

Two hours later, I got a message from Doc, asking me to call as soon as I could do so privately.

"Ready for us?"

"I'm calling a meeting of all the partners. Eighty-eight is still out of commission. Otherwise, those who aren't already here, are flying in."

"When and where?"

"This afternoon, if we can make it happen, and we're coming to you."

"Anything you can tell me in advance?"

"Negative."

"What's going on?" said Malin, who had just come down the stairs.

"K19 meeting here this afternoon."

"What about Striker?"

I told her I didn't think to ask about him. However, if he'd been in the ICU just yesterday, I doubted there would be a way the man could travel to the meeting.

"I want to talk to Burns."

"I'll see if I can find him."

When he answered my call, Burns invited us to come up to the main house for breakfast, telling me we'd talk after we ate.

"I wasn't hungry until I smelled bacon," Malin whispered when we walked in.

"Good morning," said Bradley, who was sitting, feeding a baby while Naughton sat on the arm of her chair, rubbing her neck.

"Long night without much sleep," he muttered.

"Is the baby okay?" Malin asked.

Before either of them could answer, Sorcha came out of the kitchen. "Karma," she said as she set a platter of breakfast meats on the table. "Naughton had no interest in sleeping once the sun set."

He shook his head, rolled his eyes, and looked at me. "I heard my big brother will be here later today."

"Affirmative."

"Not just him," said Sorcha. "We'll have a crowd for dinner tonight."

"Is there anything I can do to help?" Malin offered.

Sorcha leaned in closer to her. "No, lass. You'll be quite busy this afternoon," she whispered.

"It sounds like you know more than I do."

"She usually knows more than the rest of us," said Burns, walking up behind us with more platters of food.

Two more of Doc's brothers showed up with their wives and babies right after we were seated, and joined us at the table.

I kept my eye on Malin as we ate. She was subdued, as I usually was whenever I was with a large group of people. As an only child who had spent most of her life with no one other than her father, she likely felt as overwhelmed by the number of people at the table as I did.

"How are you holding up?" I asked, leaning closer to her.

She smiled. "About as well as you are."

I looked across the table at Burns, who motioned with his head for us to join him.

With all the commotion, it didn't appear that anyone saw the three of us leave the room.

"It's a beautiful day. Would you mind if we talked in the courtyard?"

I put my hand on the small of Malin's back as we followed Burns outside.

"I won't be joining you this afternoon, so I wanted to have our chat before the rest of your team arrived."

Malin nodded. "Yes, sir."

"While I don't know the details of your mission, I do have some insight into the workings of the agency before either of you were born, let alone worked there. Do you mind?" he asked, tapping his pipe on a stone and pulling a pouch of tobacco from his pocket.

"Please go ahead," Malin answered.

"Terrible habit," said Burns as he brought the pipe to his lips and lit it. "I'll get right to it," he said, and Malin nodded.

"I've known Ed Montgomery longer than I would like to have," he began.

"I concur," said Malin.

"You probably wonder what he's still doing there."

"At times I have."

"Monty is very well-connected in Washington. I've seen many directors come and go over the years, all determined to cut him loose. However, when each one left, he stayed."

"Who is he connected to?" I asked.

"While most of the old guard have died off, there are a couple of hangers-on in Congress who still control too much of the power in our nation's capital."

I knew exactly who Burns was talking about and assumed Malin did too.

"You are familiar, I'm sure, with the secret society known as Skull and Bones."

"Yes, sir."

"And you are aware of the connections from each branch of our government to the society?"

"Some," she answered. "The president, for example."

"There are also members who are in both the House and the Senate as well as sitting on the Supreme Court."

"Is Montgomery a member?" I asked.

"No, but both his father and grandfather were."

"As were the president's," Malin added.

"Exactly," said Burns. "As well as more than one former Director of the CIA."

"I hadn't heard about Montgomery's connection," said Malin.

"Few do," said Burns. "His father, Prescott Edmund Montgomery, Jr., was convicted of murder shortly before his son joined the agency. Many say the man took the fall for the crimes of another."

"Is that why Montgomery is untouchable?" she asked.

"I had no idea."

"I would've been surprised if you did. You must remember, I am far older than you are and rose through the ranks at a time when secrets were buried rather than exposed on the nightly news. However, that didn't mean they weren't talked about."

"It's hard to discern sometimes what of those rumors are fact and what are urban legend," said Malin.

"How do you think this information relates to your investigation, Special Agent Kilbourne?"

"Think, Malin," said Burns.

Her eyes met his. "The reelection was hard won. Some say it wasn't won at all."

Burns nodded, his eyes scrunched, but with an undeniable pride. "Keep going."

I held my breath, wondering if Malin would continue, or if she'd look at me. If she did, I would know that she wasn't fully ready to trust me.

She did look, but before I could stand to leave, Malin spoke.

"Could the Islamic State influence the outcome of the election?" she asked. "And why would United Russia pay Ghafor to get them to do so?"

"I don't know the answer, but I'd say you're on the right track." Burns stood and went into the house, leaving us alone in the courtyard.

"What do you think?" I asked when she didn't say anything.

"The problem is there's no proof."

"Of?"

"Money laundering or election fraud. Maybe both."

"I need a computer," Malin said as we walked back into the cottage.

When I pulled mine out of my bag, Malin's seagrass angel ornament fell to the floor.

"Here it is," she said, picking it up. "I thought I lost it." She put the string on her finger like I'd seen her do before, and twirled it while I powered up the computer and logged in with my credentials.

"I appreciate this, Dutch."

"What can I do to help?"

"Think of as many instances when the US government colluded with known enemies to achieve a seemingly unrelated goal."

There were countless examples, as disheartening as that was. Few ever came to be known by the American people, but inside the walls of the CIA, deals were made on a regular basis.

"The most well-known involve Iran," I said, pulling a notepad and pen out of my bag.

"I get it. Burns thinks this has something to do with the president getting reelected when the polls indicated he didn't have a prayer of doing so." She groaned and put her head in her hand. "But I don't know or understand the what or the why."

We spent the next two hours creating lists and then charts, drawing lines between the countries and organizations known to have made significant side deals in the last few years.

"When was Burns at the agency?" I asked.

"Officially, between 1971 and 1979."

"No shortage of political scandals then." I rolled my shoulders.

"Let's go through them and see if anything strikes us as similar."

Malin turned her head away from the computer when I didn't say anything. "Don't tell me you're hungry."

Actually, I was, but now I felt stupid saying anything.

"We can take a break," she offered.

"It's okay." I'd been on missions where I didn't eat in longer than twenty-four hours. Unfortunately doing research didn't produce the same level of adrenaline that a firefight when outnumbered by bad guys did.

"Really, it's okay."

Malin stood and walked over to the refrigerator, not that I expected there to be much in it. I watched as she pulled out a head of lettuce and then looked around the kitchen until she found a loaf of bread and some tomatoes. She went back to the refrigerator and pulled out bacon. "BLT okay?" she asked.

I probably should've gotten up to help her, but I was mesmerized, watching her instead. "Perfect."

"Why doesn't Burns just tell me what he thinks?" she asked as she put slices of bacon in a pan.

I'd wondered that myself, but the man must have a reason other than trying to get her to figure it out for herself. The woman had been working this for over a year. She didn't need a lesson in being an agent.

"The biggest political scandal of the seventies was Watergate," I said.

"There was the Strategic Arms Limitation Talks, although that was an accomplishment versus a scandal," Malin countered.

"What else along those lines?"

"Nixon ended the draft. Changed the direction of the Supreme Court. Both of those would be considered accomplishments domestically."

"What else, besides opening China?"

"He signed the Paris Peace Accords ending US involvement in the Vietnam War."

I shook my head. "Wait a minute."

Malin stopped what she was doing and looked up at me.

"We're overthinking this. Burns isn't alluding to something that happened. He's trying to tell us what to do next. What was the beginning of Nixon's downfall?"

"The money trail."

"Exactly."

# 24

*Malin*

Six hours later, I watched as the partners of K19 filed into the winery where there was a room big enough for them to meet without disrupting the family, as well as a twenty-foot-long table where the attendees could all be seated.

When I saw Kellen McTiernan and Sumner Copeland get out of one of the SUVs, the hair on the back of my neck stood up.

"Easy," said Dutch when my eyes met those of the man who had been my handler, and I visibly bristled.

"I didn't expect them."

"Neither did I."

I was even more surprised when I saw Striker Ellis walk directly over to me after getting out of the next SUV that pulled up.

"We're close," said Ellis. "Thanks entirely to you." He turned to Dutch. "We'd be even closer if you hadn't been so goddamn trigger happy."

"Good to see you too, Ellis. How are you feeling? Did the hospital psych ward release you, or did you leave against medical advice?"

"The rumors surrounding my condition were greatly exaggerated. By design."

"Good to see you, Malin," said Copeland, who continued inside when Striker motioned him by.

Ranger Messick, Diesel Jacks, and Monk Perrin got out of the same vehicle Striker had. Ranger didn't look as though he'd been shot the day before either.

"Who else are we waiting for?" asked Striker.

"Mantis and Alegria are right behind us," Ranger answered.

I felt my heart go into my throat. I was already intimidated by the people who were assembled inside, most of whom were considered legends in the intelligence business—Doc Butler, Razor Sharp, and Gunner Godet were thought to be the most effective special forces operatives in the world. But Alegria Mondreau intimidated me more than all the rest combined.

"Would you like to go inside now?" Dutch asked.

"Why? Would you prefer to talk to her alone?"

"Malin…"

"What?"

"I'm asking if you'd like to go inside with me."

"They're your closest friends, and you aren't going to greet them? How odd." Was he ashamed of me? Did he want them to think his relationship with me was purely professional?

"Come here." Dutch pulled me next to him and put his arm around my waist.

"There he is," I heard Mantis Cassman say while holding the SUV door open for Alegria.

The woman was even more beautiful than I remembered. Her exit from the vehicle was a lesson in grace. Rather than walking toward me, she appeared to be floating. Damn French. I'd never liked them.

"It's nice to see you," Alegria said directly to me after she and Dutch had hugged.

"And you," I responded. Although, really, I'd prefer to see a rattlesnake over the woman standing in front of me.

I looked over at Dutch, who was in a serious-looking conversation with Mantis.

"If you'll excuse me, I was just about to go inside."

"I'll join you," said Alegria in her perfectly irritating, exaggerated French accent.

Once we were inside, I made a beeline for Burns, hoping Alegria wouldn't follow.

"You've had some time to think," said Burns when I approached.

I looked over my shoulder to see if anyone was in hearing distance. "You're suggesting I dig deeper into the money trail."

Burns nodded and smiled.

I followed his line of sight, which brought me in direct eye contact with Kellen McTiernan.

"There you are," said Dutch, walking up to join us. "I thought you might like to say hello to Mantis."

"I can later. I wanted the chance to talk to Burns."

When I turned back around, Burns was gone. "That's weird. He was just here."

"He went out that way," said Dutch, pointing to a door I hadn't noticed near the back of the room. "If I remember correctly, he said he wouldn't be staying for the meeting."

I looked around for a place to sit that was as far from Alegria Mondreau as possible. It appeared my best bet was to stay right where I was.

"Since it doesn't look as though Doc is ready to start, I thought I'd sneak over and say hello." Mantis leaned forward and kissed both of my cheeks. How very French of him.

"Malin and Dutch, would the two of you come with me? There are some things I'd like to brief you on before we get started," said Doc, walking over to us.

Dutch held back.

"Are you coming?" I asked.

"Only if you're certain you want me to," he said, but then leaned closer. "This is your mission. Don't think I've forgotten that."

"I want you to hear whatever Doc has to say."

Dutch nodded, and we followed Doc through the door Burns had previously used. When we entered what looked like a private tasting room, I saw that McTiernan and Copeland were already seated at the table, along with Burns.

"I hope you don't mind that I asked my father to join us."

"I'm glad he's here." The other two, however, were a different story.

"In a meeting earlier today, Kellen briefed me on information that you need to be made aware of," Doc said to me.

"Agent Kilbourne," began McTiernan, "the work you have done on this mission thus far has been exemplary. What Doc alluded to in terms of the information you should be made aware of, is that I, too, have been working on the same investigation, albeit from a different direction."

Doc stepped forward. "It seems that Striker's departure from the agency was carefully timed. While his intention was to leave the CIA's employ, his departure lent itself to a strategic maneuver on the part of the NSA."

"As you are aware, Kilbourne, my expertise is in analysis, specifically relating to signal evaluation and trafficking, but more importantly, money," said McTiernan.

I nodded. "Go on."

"While you stumbled on a particular money trail all on your own, a team at the NSA did as well, but more than six months after you did."

"That's when Striker resigned," said Dutch, looking between Doc and McTiernan. "Your code name makes a lot more sense now."

The agent known to some as "Money" was rarely referred to as such. Some names stuck; others didn't. I had hated the code name "Starling" the first time it was used in reference to me, and refused to even answer to it.

"As I told Doc earlier, the ambush you heard about was a setup designed to lead some of our higher-ranking agents to believe Ghafor was assassinated."

My eyes opened wide. "He's alive?"

"He is, and is in a secure location, awaiting his interview with you, Kilbourne," said Doc.

"What have you learned from him?" I asked McTiernan directly.

"Nothing. He's refusing to talk to anyone but you."

I tamped down the reflex to smile until I looked at Dutch, who winked.

"I wish I could tell you that Orlov is alive as well," said McTiernan, looking at Dutch. "Sadly, at least for this particular mission, he is not. However, I don't question your motives, sir."

Dutch nodded, but didn't speak.

"What's the next step, after I meet with Ghafor?"

McTiernan didn't immediately answer. Instead, he looked at Doc.

"Montgomery."

# 25

*Dutch*

I recognized two things—the tone of Doc's voice and the look on his face, and I didn't like either.

"You're going to bait him."

Doc nodded. "That's the plan we'll be presenting to the team when we go back in."

"Who?" I asked, already knowing the answer.

"Malin would be the only logical choice."

When I stood, the chair I'd been sitting in almost hit the floor. If the wall behind me weren't made of stone, I would've put my fist through it in an effort to stop myself from saying something I knew I'd regret. Instead, I paced. I couldn't even look at Malin, knowing what I'd see would be disappointment in my reaction.

"Why Montgomery specifically?" I asked.

"I'll answer if you don't mind," said Cope, looking between Doc and McTiernan before turning to Malin.

"First, since Kellen didn't tell you what I'm doing here, I want you to know that I've been tracking you since you arrived in Germany."

I looked at Malin, whose face paled.

"I was aware of your movement and of the intercepted conversations and made sure throughout that no one else was, other than McTiernan."

"You're saying I wasn't on my own quite as much as I believed I was."

Copeland nodded.

"Thank you."

"What were you going to say about Montgomery?" I asked, growing increasingly impatient.

"He's the loosest of the cannons in an arsenal hierarchy that is…terrifying."

I wanted to take Cope by the throat and tell him to stop talking in fucking metaphors and answer my damn question. Instead, I met Malin's gaze and reined myself in.

"Malin," said Doc. "The NSA has found evidence that Montgomery controlled the Super PAC. As you know, the money transfer was carefully timed."

"The reporting deadline was after the election."

"That's right. And the Super PAC was dissolved prior to that deadline as well."

"Making it almost impossible to track the money going in or out."

McTiernan spoke up. "If you hadn't made the connection to Ghafor and brought in Orlov, they would've gotten away with it."

"With what?" she asked.

"We aren't one hundred percent certain at this point, but whatever it is, has to do with the presidential election."

"Do you have enough evidence to get the attorney general to appoint a special prosecutor?" I asked.

"No. That's where Montgomery comes in," answered Doc. "He needs to believe that Malin does, and is about to act on it."

I knew that what Doc was proposing was part of Malin's job. She'd been trained to handle these types of situations. In fact, what she'd accomplished in the last year required her to put herself in far more dangerous ones. The difference now was, I would be aware of it.

I had no business voicing my opinion, but then, I had no business being in this meeting. Doc never should've included me, and I shouldn't have agreed.

"Your plan is to get him to give everyone else up." What I didn't say was that would happen only if they stopped Montgomery from killing Malin first.

He won't take the fall alone," said Burns, who had remained quiet up to that point. "He's not the man his father was."

I looked at Doc. "I have a question."

"I'm sure you have many."

"What about the DHS guy who uncovered all of this? How did he die?"

"Car accident," answered Cope. "Or something intended to look like one."

I turned my back and rolled my shoulders.

"Can I speak with Dutch alone?" Malin asked.

"Of course," said Doc.

He, McTiernan, and Copeland stood, but Burns stayed where he was.

"Dad?" said Doc.

Burns nodded. "I'll join you in a moment."

Once the three men left the room, Burns stood. "I'll just say this." He looked at me. "Montgomery needs to be taken down, but it goes much deeper than just him. Everything I believe in, have fought my whole life for, is at risk. The very principles this nation was founded on are threatened." With that, Burns walked out.

I understood what the man meant. I also respected what it took for him to say the words out loud. If it were anyone other than Malin putting herself at risk, I wouldn't have questioned the op that Doc was proposing.

I closed my eyes. I could see the plan Doc would lay out once we went back in and briefed the team. It would be airtight. Malin would be protected from every angle, but that didn't stop me from wishing I could volunteer to take her place.

I opened my eyes and looked into hers.

"Dutch?"

I sat down and took her hands in mine. "I'm struggling."

"I know you are, but this is something I have to do."

"I understand. I just don't like it."

"Do you have another idea?"

I shook my head. "It's your mission, Malin. You have to see it through."

"I'm only going to ask one thing of you."

"Jesus," I said, scrubbing my face with my hand. "What?"

"Don't shoot Montgomery until he's through testifying."

"Until he's through?"

Malin smiled. "After that, I don't care what happens to him."

I cupped her cheek. "You're something else. You know that, right? Think about all the men and women sitting out in that other room. You're just as badass as every single one of them, if not more so."

"I think you're overstating—"

"You heard McTiernan. He said it took an entire team at the NSA to figure out what you did all on your own. The damn head of the Islamic State won't talk to anyone but you. You even had Sergei Orlov eating out of the palm of your hand."

"Until you killed him."

"Yeah, yeah. I hear you and everyone else loud and clear. I get it. Don't kill anyone else until they've testified."

# 26

*Malin*

"Can everyone please take a seat?" asked Doc, looking around the room.

I surveyed the people seated at the table. Other than Merrigan and Alegria, I was the only woman here.

"I want to thank you all for changing whatever plans you may have had in order to join us here today."

Onyx shifted over a seat so I could be seated between Dutch and Doc.

"Along with all but one of the K19 senior partners, who happens to be my son-in-law, all of our junior partners are here. Thank you, ladies and gentlemen." Doc made eye contact with each of them.

"We have two men joining us who have been part of the mission we're about to discuss, and I don't think I'm speaking out of turn when I say that we'd like to bring both of them on board as soon as they're ready." Doc motioned to Ranger and Diesel. "You all know Messick and Jacks." Doc cleared his throat. "Now, for the reason I called you all here."

I listened as Doc gave a brief overview of the mission I'd originally been assigned.

"What started out as an infiltration designed to bring down the Islamic State, turned into an investigation that the K19 team has recently gotten involved in. Special Agent Kilbourne will brief you about what she's uncovered."

I told those in the room about the money coming into Super PAC, and then about the trail of payments that I believed went back out to Ghafor.

"The ramifications of what we have discovered may be far-reaching and involve our own government." I looked around the room as those there sat quietly, paying attention to every word I said.

When I was finished, I asked McTiernan what his role in all this had been, along with Copeland's. When he'd completed his portion of the briefing, Doc asked for questions.

"I worked with Montgomery," said Gunner. "Slimy *sonuvabitch*. Whatever you decide to do, I'm in."

"Me too," said Razor.

"You've told us what you've uncovered, which doesn't add up to much except money changing hands," said Alegria, looking directly at me. "You mentioned the ramifications could be far-reaching. Meaning what exactly?"

I heard Dutch mutter but didn't catch exactly what he said. I had no problem answering Alegria's question, or anyone else's. Whether she liked the answer or not, wasn't my problem.

"What I believe the far-reaching ramifications to be is irrelevant at this time. Anything other than finding a way to get Agent Montgomery to confess his involvement, as well as name the others involved in what appears to be a conspiracy, is premature."

Before Alegria could say anything else. Doc stepped forward.

"Most of you know my father, Burns Butler. If you haven't met him before today, I'm sure you've heard of him. I want to share with you what I overheard him say a few minutes ago."

Doc had the attention of everyone in the room. "I'm going to quote him verbatim. He said, 'Montgomery needs to be taken down, but it goes much deeper than just him. Everything I believe in, have fought my whole life for, is at risk. The very principles this nation was founded on are threatened.'"

He looked around the room. "You may be wondering why I remember it word for word. My father doesn't say anything that doesn't need to be said. Kind of like Monk over there."

When Monk bowed his head in acknowledgment, most in the room laughed.

"When Burns does speak, those within hearing distance are wise to listen. Now, I'm going to ask Gunner and Razor to meet with Kilbourne, Striker, and McTiernan to put a plan together. Dutch and Copeland, you can join them. Everyone else, sit tight, have a glass of wine. If you're hungry, I'm sure my mother has prepared enough food to feed three times as many as are here. That's if Dutch doesn't eat."

Dutch flipped him off as he pulled my chair out. "Again, it's your call. If you don't want me in there, I'll hang out."

"Are you going to try to talk me out of—"

"No," he said before I could finish. "And that display from earlier, I won't repeat it."

"Thank you."

Dutch put his hand on the small of my back as we followed Gunner and Razor back to the room we'd met in earlier.

"By the way, I don't know what that crap with Alegria was about earlier. I can talk to her."

I shook my head. "It's not necessary."

"Let me know if you change your mind."

"Dutch, I can handle myself with her. I don't need you to intervene."

He nodded and followed me into the room where the others were waiting.

# 27

*Dutch*

"I don't know how the hell you rank high enough to be in here. Any of the three of you," Gunner said to me, Striker, and Copeland.

I knew he was joking, but Cope looked uncomfortable and Striker looked pissed. On the other hand, Striker always had a scowl on his face.

"Here's how I see it," said Razor. "This is Kilbourne's mission, so instead of Gunner and me figuring out how she wants to run it, let's let her do it."

Malin stood. "To recap, everyone from the agency, outside of the two of you, believes Ghafor is dead."

"That's correct," answered McTiernan.

"What about Striker and Ranger?"

"As far as the agency is concerned, both are still in the hospital in varying degrees of critical condition."

"And the two dead men?"

"Didn't exist to begin with."

"We need Montgomery to think that Ghafor fed me both proof and details while I was still in Pakistan.

Same with Orlov. That he read me in before he was killed."

"Montgomery will have questions before he acts," said Striker.

Malin nodded. "What else we can dangle as bait will be based on how much Ghafor knows. He may know it all, even whether United Russia is involved in the way I think they were."

I couldn't remember a time I felt as proud as I did at that moment. Malin Kilbourne was kick-ass good at what she did. Given she'd worked for me early in her career, I gave myself a little pat on the back, but the reality was, it was all her.

It would be a damn shame if she retired at the end of this mission like she'd told me she planned to when we were in South Carolina. The world would lose one of the "good guys," someone smart enough, brave enough, and savvy enough to take down the Islamic State, the corrupt parts of the Central Intelligence Agency, Congress, and maybe even neutralize the bad guys in the executive and judicial branches of the US government.

And United Russia? She might be able to hit them hard enough that they'd stop believing they could poke their nose into the inner-workings of America.

"Timeline?" asked McTiernan.

"Depends on when you're leaving," muttered Gunner. "Now probably wouldn't be too soon."

The agent leveled his gaze at the K19 senior partner. "I'll remind you that your fiancée might very well have a bounty on her head if I hadn't been part of the team that negotiated its release. Before you dismiss me, keep that in mind."

Gunner threw his head back and laughed. "Well, look who finally showed up. Quit pussyfooting around, McTiernan. No one here is going to treat you with respect unless you prove yourself worthy of it."

If it had been me, I would've told Gunner to fuck off, which would've probably made him respect me more. McTiernan just stared him down.

"You get used to it," Striker told his replacement. "You went to college. Hazing doesn't end once you have a degree."

"Pussy," everyone in the room heard Gunner mumble, followed by Striker flipping him off.

This was standard procedure when the entire K19 team met, but as the only woman in the room, I wondered what Malin thought of them.

When I looked over at her, she had her head buried in my computer and didn't seem to be paying attention to any of them.

"Hey, can we get Kilbourne her own technology sometime soon?"

McTiernan nodded. "I have a complete setup with me. Give me a hand, Copeland?"

I watched as Malin's handler and McTiernan left the room.

"He's hella smart," Razor said once they were gone. "You might want to remember that too. Kinda like not insulting the waiter at a restaurant."

Gunner nodded but didn't bother hiding his smirk.

Once McTiernan and Copeland returned with a phone, computer, and gun for Malin, it took us less than thirty minutes to craft our plan.

Razor leaned back in his chair and put his hands behind his head. "I like watchin' the youngins do all the work, don't you, Gunner?"

"Until shit gets real. Then it takes the old guys to come to the rescue."

It wasn't that long ago that I was being held captive by someone loosely connected to al-Qaeda who had an equally loose connection with sanity. If it weren't for Razor and Doc, I might've died at the hands of Zamed Safi. I'd never take the "old guys" for granted.

"If we're done here, I'd be up for finding out what kind of food Doc promised Sorcha was preparing."

Malin smiled and shook her head. "Let's go, then. We wouldn't want you to starve to death."

I hung back while the rest of the men filtered out of the room.

"I'm damn proud of you, Malin. I want you to know it, too."

Her cheeks turned pink, and she smiled. "That means a lot to me, Dutch."

"I don't think I've ever been prouder of anyone."

"Yeah?" she said, wrapping her arms around my neck. "Not even the French pilot?"

I bent my head and kissed her. "Not remotely close."

Malin pressed her tongue against my lips, and I opened to her while, at the same time, lifting her up so her body rested against mine. "I want to be alone with you," I muttered against her lips.

"More than you want to eat?"

"I don't think those two things are mutually exclusive," I answered, wiggling my eyebrows.

"Come on," she said, pulling me from the room by the hand. "The sooner we get some food in you, the sooner we can politely excuse ourselves and be alone."

"I like the sound of that."

# 28

*Malin*

When we walked out, the winery's tasting bar was covered with platters of food, and a lot more people had arrived than were there earlier.

I recognized Doc's brother Naughton and his wife, Bradley, as well as his other two brothers, Maddox and Brodie, and their wives. I remembered Burns saying something about the two women running a tasting room together in Cambria, which was on the coast.

Once this mission was over and I retired, maybe I'd have more time to visit places like the seaside village. I looked over at Dutch, who was surrounded by the rest of the K19 junior partners, talking and laughing. I smiled at how much fun he appeared to be having. When he looked over and I waved, he winked and held up a finger.

I shook my head. I was in no hurry to take him away from the men he probably didn't get to spend much downtime with. I'd love to have that kind of camaraderie with people I worked with, but I wasn't very good at it.

Looking around the room, I saw Merrigan talking with her sisters-in-law, all of them holding babies on their laps. I didn't know much about the backgrounds of anyone other than Merrigan, who had once been the top pick for managing director of MI6. Talk about badass, and yet here she was, married, with a baby, sitting around and laughing.

Could that be my life one day? Dutch and I were so far away from anything remotely resembling a committed relationship. And even if we did continue to spend time together once this mission was over, I had no idea how he felt about things like marriage or having children.

Neither of us had a great example to follow in terms of our parents' relationships. My mother had left me and my father when I was so young, I never remembered her being around at all.

Dutch's father had died, and it sounded like his stepfather was abusive to the point where Dutch had left and never looked back. Maybe that experience had turned him into a non-believer in marriage. It certainly made me think twice about whether a traditional relationship could ever work for me.

"Your longing is showing," said Alegria, walking up behind me.

"You don't know me well enough to read my expressions or have any idea what I might be thinking about."

"One wouldn't have to know a thing about you to see what is clearly written all over your face."

I folded my arms and turned so my back was facing where Dutch was standing. "This may surprise you, but I have no interest in getting to know you better, or even having this conversation."

"Dutch is very special to me."

I glared at her. "And?"

"I want to see him with someone worthy of the man he is."

I shook my head and walked away. I was almost out the door when Dutch intercepted me.

"Where are you going?"

"I need some fresh air. I have a headache."

Dutch put his hand on the small of my back, like he did so often, and steered me toward the door. "Let's go, then."

"I don't want to take you away from your friends. I'll just go lie down for a bit and see if my headache goes away."

"What happened in there?" he asked once we were outside.

"Nothing."

"I saw you talking to Alegria. Tell me what she said."

I sighed. "Your ex-girlfriend wants to be sure you're with someone worthy of your wonderfulness. Evidently, I don't measure up."

Dutch spun me around and rested his hands on my shoulders. "I'm the one in this relationship who doesn't measure up."

"Look, we aren't in a—"

Dutch gripped the back of my neck and covered my mouth with his, kissing me in that way he did that made my knees go weak. His other hand came up and cupped my cheek. His tongue wound its way around mine, and he ground his hardness into me. Pulling back, he rested his forehead against mine.

"I don't know what you were going to say, but if it was that we aren't in a relationship, then we need to talk."

"We should wait until this is all over and see how we feel then, Dutch."

"Nothing is going to change for me, Malin, because I am in a relationship with you. When the mission ends, you and I will figure out together what we want to do next. The only thing I'm not willing to do, is let you go again."

I tried to shake my head, but his grip was too tight.

"I'm crazy about you, baby. I can't get enough of you, and I don't think that will ever change."

"There's more to life than sex, Dutch."

"Yeah? Well, there's more on the menu than spaghetti and meatballs too. It just so happens that that's my favorite thing to eat. Doesn't mean I'm never going to eat anything else."

I laughed. "That is a terrible analogy. Or are you saying that I'm your favorite, like spaghetti, but that doesn't mean you aren't going to see other people?"

"You can't be serious."

"Remember this is all pretend, Dutch. When life goes back to whatever normal is for you and me, neither of us may want to continue spending this much time together."

He put one arm behind my knees, the other around my waist, and lifted me off my feet. He carried me over to the swing on the porch of the main house.

When he sat, he kept me on his lap. "I'll remind you that I offered to buy you an island. Would I have done that if I didn't want to spend every day and night with you?"

"You weren't serious."

"Wasn't I? You sure about that? Are you sure that I haven't already talked to Doc, Gunner, and Razor about it?"

"Have you?"

"You're damn right I have."

"That's for you, Dutch."

He brought his hand back up to cup my cheek and looked into my eyes. "No, Malin, it isn't for me. It's for us. You may not want to spend all your time with me, and I guess I'll just have to accept that. But for me, twenty-four hours a day, seven days a week sounds just about as perfect as I could imagine."

I moved my head back just slightly, and Dutch dropped his hand.

"I know how easy it is to get caught up in everything that's going on in there. Marriages, babies, people who were once independent no longer being so, but tomorrow, when everyone goes back home and it's just you and me, will the allure of doing what everyone else is, still be so attractive?"

"I have no idea what you just said, or what it means. I don't give a shit what anyone inside that winery, or even anyone else in the world, is doing. I want to be with you. That's it."

"You can honestly say that Mantis and Alegria's engagement has nothing to do with you wanting to be with me? As she'll be all too happy to remind me, you mean a lot to her and she intends to look out for you."

Dutch stood back up with me still in his arms and walked back toward the winery.

"Put me down. I don't know what you're about to do, but I beg you, please don't."

Dutch kept walking.

"Don't do this," I said again, trying to wiggle out of his arms.

Once he got to the door, he set me on my feet.

"I'm asking you to come back inside with me. I won't force you, but I'd really like it if you would."

"What are you going to do?"

"We're gonna play a trivia game—the Dutch Miller version."

# 29

*Dutch*

I walked in, holding Malin's hand, and looked around the room until I spotted Mantis and Alegria. With her hand firmly in mine, I led her over to where they were seated.

"Hey, Mantis, Al," I said, using a shortened version of her code name that she detested. "I feel like Malin and I haven't had five minutes to catch up with you two."

"Alegria was just wondering where you'd run off to," said Mantis with a glint in his eye that told me he knew I was up to something. "How's life been, brother?"

I laughed. "I'd say it's been pretty good since I got out of the hellhole we call the Middle East. How about you?"

"Same," said Mantis, covering Alegria's hand with his. "We're working on getting Manon's clearance to fly."

"That's great, Al," I said, looking straight at her. Just like I could've predicted, she was glaring at me, and

Malin's expression wasn't much better. "How are the wedding plans coming along?"

"Do you want to tell them or should I?" Mantis asked his fiancée.

"I'm sure they're not interested."

"Not interested?" I clutched my heart. "Are you saying you've replaced me as best man? Do you know how much work I've already done, planning the games for the wedding shower? Those are co-ed these days, right?"

Mantis laughed. "I'm curious why you know that."

"I pay attention to shit like that."

"Sure you do. This oughta be good. What kind of games?"

"Let's see...plant a kiss on Mantis. That's where we blow up a giant photo of you, and all the ladies take turns kissing it to see who gets closest to your lips."

"I'd be willing to try that live, meaning no picture," he said, wiggling his eyebrows at Alegria and Malin.

When that got no reaction, Mantis encouraged me to go on.

"What about who knows the most about the groom? Bet I could win that one."

"You don't know him better than I do," said Alegria, taking my bait.

"No? Wanna bet? Let's see who among the three of us knows the other two the best."

"How do you propose we do that?"

"We need a couple of pieces of paper. Four, in fact." I walked up to the bar and grabbed four tasting sheets and pens.

"I hope you're not suggesting I play along. I don't know much about any of you," said Malin.

"You just write down your answers for me, baby," I said, leaning over to kiss her cheek.

"Let's get started. This is how it'll work. Malin will answer just for me. I'll answer for Mantis and Alegria. Al, you answer for me and Mantis. Get the picture?"

"Yes, I get the picture," she spat. "And don't call me that."

I smiled. "First question. Favorite food." I took a minute to write down my answer for my two friends, and waited until they were finished before I went on.

"Next. How many siblings do each of us have?"

Again, I paused.

"Ready?" I asked when Alegria set her pen down.

"I don't find this amusing, Dutch."

"Yeah, well, I don't care. Drop out if you feel like it." I didn't bother trying to hide the sneer in my voice. She should've left Malin the hell alone if she didn't want to deal with my wrath.

"Next question. If we could travel anywhere in the world we wanted to, what would be number one on the list?"

Mantis, sitting beside me, was chuckling, but only loud enough for me to hear him.

"Last question, this one might be TMI, but if we could spend our time doing one thing, above everything else, what would that be?"

Instead of chuckling, Mantis burst out laughing.

"This isn't funny," said Alegria, throwing her pen at him.

Mantis scooted his chair closer to hers. "Let me see your answers."

"No," she said, putting her hand over what she'd written.

"I'm changing the rules of this game. Instead of the groom, let's see who knows the best man better than anyone else."

"First question. Al, what did you write down for me?"

She glared at me and didn't say anything. I turned to Mantis.

"What did you get?"

"Favorite thing to eat—burgers."

I made a noise like a buzzer. "Nope. Malin?"

At first, I thought she wasn't going to answer, but then she smiled. "Spaghetti and meatballs."

I leaned closer and kissed her cheek, murmuring in her ear. "Whose?"

When she said "mine," the little spot on her neck I loved so much, turned red.

"That's right. One for Malin, zip for Mantis and Al."

Mantis laughed again. "Knock it off, Dutch," he said, smiling. "You're proving your point."

"Let's skip number two. I'm curious, though, what did Alegria get for number three?"

"I don't think you're the least bit funny."

"Yeah, well, that really isn't the point of the game. Malin, what about you?"

"Cokabow Island."

"Ding, ding, ding. We have a winner," I said, kissing her cheek.

"Final question. What would I be doing if I could do whatever I wanted?"

Malin didn't wait for me to look at her. "Eating," she blurted. "This was too easy."

"I guess what we've learned from this little game is that maybe we don't know each other as well as we think we do, which means that maybe we don't have any idea what's best for each other either."

"Dutch," warned Mantis.

"No, I'm going to finish what I have to say. You," I said, looking straight at Alegria, "stay out of my personal life unless I invite you into it."

I knew I was being hard on her, but part of me didn't care. She had no business getting in Malin's face about anything, but she had.

"Apologize."

"I beg your pardon?"

"You heard me, Alegria. Apologize to Malin."

"Dutch, this really isn't necessary." Malin rested her hand on mine.

"It is to me."

Mantis pulled back and looked between them. "What happened?"

"You wanna tell him, or do you want me to?"

"I'm not going to apologize for wanting the best for you, Dutch. We've known each other a long time—"

"And yet, you know nothing about me. Apologize."

Alegria turned to Malin. "I'm sorry."

"Thank you," I said, standing and pulling Malin's chair out. "I'll RSVP for your wedding right here and right now. I'll be there, and Malin will be my date. Any problem with that? I didn't think so. Let's go, Malin."

"Wait a minute," said Mantis, standing too.

"What?"

He came around the table and hugged me first, and then Malin.

"If there's anything I can do to help with Abdul Ghafor, let me know. Although I think you may have a better relationship with him than I do at this point."

Malin laughed. "At this point?"

"Sounds like you know more about his feelings than I do."

Malin put her hand on Mantis' arm. "Let's just say that if Abdul finds out you're here, one of two things may happen. First, he may refuse to talk at all. The other possibility is that the third world war will break out."

Mantis laughed like Malin had. "Enough said." He leaned forward. "Godspeed."

"Thank you," Malin answered.

"Unless you need us, we're heading out."

I walked around to the other side of the table and pulled Alegria's chair out. She stood and put her arms around me.

"I care about you," she whispered. "I want you to be happy."

"I know you do, but Malin is the last person you need to worry about making me happy. She does with every breath she takes."

Alegria squeezed me hard and let go.

"Please, Al, make this right," I whispered.

She didn't look happy about it, but Alegria walked around me to where Malin stood.

"I am sorry. I've known these two since we were teenagers, which sometimes feels like they belong to me. Only one does now. The other belongs to you."

Malin thanked her and looked at me. "Should we say goodnight to the others?"

"Let's do that. I'm ready to call it a night. Take care, sweetheart," I said, kissing Alegria's cheek. "You too," I said to Mantis, waving as we walked away.

"I'm sorry I put you on the spot like that. I didn't plan for it to be more than a joke, but it didn't play out as funny as I thought it would."

"You weren't very nice to her."

"No? Well, she shouldn't have called you out in front of a room full of people. There isn't anyone here, Mantis included, who doesn't think she was out of line."

I saw Doc sitting with both of his brothers and their three wives and led Malin over to them. When he saw us approach, he stood.

"We'll see you both in the morning," he said and then turned to Malin. "Damn good work, Kilbourne. I don't know what your future holds, but I sure would like to see you on our team."

Merrigan stood and put her hand on Malin's arm. "I would too. You're a fine agent and a very brave human being."

"I'm Alex," said one of the other two women. "I don't know if you remember me, and I have no idea what Kade and Merrigan are talking about, but I know this; as badass as you sound, you'd fit in around here just perfectly. Wouldn't she, Peyton?"

The other woman smiled and nodded. "Definitely."

"What're you thinkin', Dutch?" asked Doc. "Maybe considering a move to the West Coast? Oh wait, there's a little island off the coast of South Carolina with your name on it, isn't there?"

"We'll see. Right now, Malin and I are taking each day as they come."

# 30

*Malin*

When we got outside the winery door, Dutch lifted my hair from my neck and kissed me.

"What's going on, Dutch?"

"What do you mean?"

"That was fun and all, but aren't you being more than a little presumptuous?"

"I have no idea what you're talking about."

I closed my eyes and took a deep breath. Was he really that thickheaded or was he dismissing me? "'Malin and I are taking each day as they come,' or how about 'I'll RSVP for your wedding right now. I'll be there, and Malin will be my date.'"

"What about it?" he asked as we walked to the cottage.

"What if I don't want to go to a wedding with you?"

"You don't?"

"That's my point. You don't know if I want to or not, because you didn't ask me."

"I'm sorry, I just assumed…"

I stopped walking. "Dutch?"

He stopped too. "I'm sorry, okay? I got a little ahead of myself."

"A little?"

"I really don't see what the problem is, Malin."

"A few days ago, you shot a man who was holding me at gunpoint and forced me to flee an op I was in the midst of. If you remember, I did not go along with you willingly. Not only that, but in that same time period, we've argued as much as we've had sex."

"I haven't made a secret of the fact that I want you in my life."

"No, you haven't, but I haven't said that's what I want."

"Yes, you did."

"When?"

"'Oh, Dutch, can't we pretend this is our life for just a little while?'"

"Are you mocking me?"

"I'm repeating what you said to me, Malin."

"Tell me, once this op is done, how do you see us?"

"I don't know. Taking some time off, going back to the island, figuring out what life might look like for us."

"You've decided all of this without consulting me."

"Hold on a minute. I said I didn't know."

"What if I see us going our separate ways?"

Dutch opened the front door of the cottage and motioned for me to go in ahead of him. "Is that really what you see happening?"

"Are you really asking me to make a decision about my future when I'm in the middle of the most important thing I've ever done? I mean, could you imagine if I'd showed up in Somalia when you were on your way to extract Mantis from the pirates, and I said, 'Hey, Dutch? What do you say we move in together when this is all over?'"

"It's a little different."

"Is it? Are you under the impression that I don't need to stay as focused as you had to be under those circumstances? Are you also under the impression that I'm not fighting for my life?"

"I think you're exaggerating the situation."

I couldn't believe my ears. "I want you to leave."

"Leave? Where am I supposed to go?"

"I don't know, but I don't want you here."

"What does that mean, exactly? Leave the cottage, leave the ranch, or leave your life?"

"For now, the cottage."

"Jesus, Malin. Hold on a minute…"

"No, Dutch. I can't be around you right now."

# 31

*Dutch*

I stood by the front door and watched Malin walk up the stairs. What the hell had just happened? One minute I was kissing the back of her neck, and the next she was kicking me out of bed.

There was no point in arguing with her now, so I walked out the door and back over to the winery.

"What are you doing here?" asked Onyx, who was standing just inside the front door. "I thought I saw you leave with the beautiful Miss Malin."

"What the fuck, Onyx? You got a thing for Malin? 'Cause the way I see it, she's with me."

"Whoa, whoa, whoa," he said, holding up his hands. "What did I do?"

"Quit with the 'beautiful Miss Malin' shit, okay?"

"Not a problem. Why don't you tell me what's turned you into such an asshole?"

I walked over to the bar, wishing they had something behind it stronger than wine. Onyx came around and picked up a bottle.

"You want some of this?" he said, holding up what looked like a bottle of red wine. "Or this?" He held up bourbon.

"I love you so much right now."

"It's a damn fine line between love and hate with you, bro."

"You know I hate it when you use that expression, *bro*."

"Seriously? Damn, man. Show your brother some love. Ain't we brothers? I sure saved your ass enough times to be considered part of your family."

"I think you're remembering things backwards. I saved your ass."

"If that's the case, then, hell, I'll call you whatever I want because, to me, you are my brother."

I rolled my shoulders. "Sorry, man. Malin just kicked me to the curb."

"Seriously?"

"You use that word too much, and yeah, she asked me to leave."

"The country?"

"Even I don't go that far. Although maybe I did. I asked her if she meant the cottage or her life."

"What did she say?"

"The cottage. For now."

"What did you do?"

"I assumed she wanted to be with me as much as I want to be with her."

"Any sentence that starts with 'I assumed' never ends well."

"I thought she and I were on the same page."

"Before Islamabad, when's the last time you saw Malin?"

"The night I went and picked Alegria up at the bar. I guess you could say it was the night we broke up."

*"Seriously?"*

"There you go again. Quit saying 'seriously.' And actually, I saw her in Germany, but I had amnesia and didn't know who she was."

"It took you a minute to go from *adios* to assuming she'd marry you, bro. What did you expect?"

"I didn't ask her to *marry* me. Although I did think she'd go to Mantis and Alegria's wedding with me."

"Still, with a woman as fine as Malin...hehe, just bustin' your balls a little there. Anyway, how would you feel, bein' jerked around like that?"

"Where are you staying?"

"Upstairs in Doc's old apartment, why?"

"Does it have more than one bedroom?"

"I think it has three."

"You've got yourself a roommate."

"Okay, but don't bitch tomorrow morning if I wake you up at dawn."

"Why are you getting up at dawn?"

"Naughton asked me if I wanted to ride. All the flying I've been doing, I feel like it's been a month since I've been on a horse."

"I didn't know you rode horses."

"Rode horses? My family contracts stock for rodeos."

"What does that mean?"

"It means he was born on the back of a horse," said Maddox's wife, as they were walking past us. "Snapper and Kick are home, and I think Trev is too if you want to meet up with them while you're in town."

"Wait, do you two know each other?" I asked.

Onyx shook his head. "Alex is my cousin, bro."

*"Seriously?"*

Onyx laughed. "Yeah, I see what you did right there."

He walked out with Alex and Maddox while I went to pour myself another glass of bourbon. Several of the partners, including Mantis and Alegria, had already left. Gunner and Razor were still there, talking to Doc and Merrigan.

"I didn't expect to see you back tonight," said Merrigan when I walked over to join them.

"Yeah, I'm in the doghouse."

She laughed. "Uh-oh. Have a seat."

I listened as they told stories about missions that happened long before I hooked up with them. Would this be me and Mantis someday? Would Alegria join in, and more importantly, would I still be the fucking odd man out? God, I was sick of being that guy. Especially when there was a woman I loved being with, sleeping alone in a bed that was only a few yards away from where I sat.

I would give just about anything to be next to her in that bed right now, feeling her skin on mine.

"What did you do?" Merrigan leaned in and asked.

"I think I may have taken her for granted."

"Go apologize, and then stay the hell out of her way."

I laughed. "She told me to leave, though."

"Listen to me."

I nodded.

"Do you think it was easy for Doc to step aside and let me finish my last mission?"

I shook my head. I'd been a part of it, on the K19 side, so I knew damn well how hard it had been for my boss.

"Your strength as a man is measured more in how you're able to keep yourself from interfering than it is if you continue to believe you have to save her. She doesn't need you to save her, Dutch."

I looked around, making sure no one was listening to our conversation and leaned forward like she had. "It wasn't that as much as it was me wanting her to commit to a life with me."

"Give her some time. She's in the middle of the most important mission she's ever undertaken. More important than most of us have."

"My head knows that, but my heart…"

"You want to save her."

I nodded again.

"Malin knows that. She watches you, you know, to see how you'll react. Sometimes it appears she's holding her breath, hoping you'll stay quiet."

I laughed out loud. "That is damn hard for me to do. God, I…"

"You care about her."

"I do, and right now I'd be willing to do just about anything to tell her that."

"And I'd be willing to bet that glass of bourbon that she's lying in that bed, wishing you were with her."

"I don't know about that. She was clear she wanted me to leave."

"Trust me on this one, and go now before you have another drink."

I left my still-full glass on the table. "Thanks, Fatale."

"My pleasure," she said, downing the bourbon.

# 32

*Malin*

I'd gone from furious to wondering what in the hell was wrong with me. What had Dutch done that was so awful? Yeah, maybe he was a little over the top with this make-believe life he was creating for the two of us, but he was right; I'd wanted to pretend for a little while too.

As much as I knew I should get out of bed and walk back over to the winery to apologize, I didn't feel like getting dressed. Even getting out of the cozy bed to find my phone and send him a text was too much for me.

My body and my brain were both so tired. The only time I'd slept well in as long as I could remember was when Dutch was in bed beside me. And what had I done? I'd sent him away.

Where was he now? In the winery with Mantis and Alegria, talking about the good old days when they were the three amigos? He'd probably even told Frenchie that I'd asked him to leave, proving her right.

I groaned and threw the covers off, feeling around for the switch on the bedside lamp. Even if I couldn't show my face, I had to at least text him and tell him I was sorry.

I froze when I heard the door open at the foot of the stairs and cursed myself for how much I'd let my guard down. I looked around, saw where I'd laid the gun McTiernan had issued me, and switched off the light.

"Malin?" I heard Dutch say. "Don't shoot, baby. It's just me."

I switched the light back on, grabbed the throw that was across the end of the bed, and wrapped it around my naked body.

"Come in," I said when I heard him knock on the bedroom door. He walked in with his hands raised.

"I'm not going to shoot you," I said, pushing back on the bed and resting against the headboard. "I was just about to text you."

Dutch sat on the bed, next to me. "What were you going to say?"

"I was going to ask you to come back."

"Yeah? What else?"

"I was going to ask if you'd consider sleeping with me."

Dutch reached around, pulled his shirt over his head, and tossed it on the floor. He leaned forward and moved my hand away from where I clasped the blanket, and spread it open.

"You are the most beautiful woman I've ever seen, Malin." He came closer and flicked my right nipple with his tongue and pinched the left between two fingers.

"Your body"—he moved his head and covered my left nipple with his lips—"was made for mine."

My head fell back against the headboard, and I weaved my fingers into Dutch's hair.

"Tell me you forgive me," he said as he scattered kisses from my breasts, up my neck, to my lips. "Tell me you want me here with you."

"I do," I said, holding his face in my hands. "I'm sorry, Dutch."

"Shh, don't be. Sometimes I'm pretty thickheaded. All you gotta do is give me a swift kick, and I'll fall back in line."

I smiled. "I'd never kick you, Dutch."

"Maybe you should, if it gets us to make-up sex faster."

"Okay, I'll think about it, but only if you take your pants off."

He stood and dropped his pants on the floor, stepped out of them, and climbed in next to me.

"Mmm, you feel so good," he groaned, resting his head between my breasts. "This is it for me, baby. I can't imagine not being right here, next to you, every single night for the rest of my life. I'm sorry if that upsets you, but it's the God's honest truth."

He sat up and rolled me over, so he was where I had been and I was sitting on his lap. As he kissed me, my hands went from his face, down his neck, and over his shoulders. He weaved his fingers with mine and held on tight.

"Open your eyes, Malin. I need you to look at me."

My gaze shifted between his eyes and mouth.

"You gotta stop doing that for a minute," he groaned. "I want you so bad it hurts."

I bent my head and kissed him.

"Malin, baby, please…"

I licked his bottom lip, raised my head, and smiled. "Sorry."

"I know I haven't handled any of this the right way, but you have to know that this isn't a mission for me. It's you and me. Us. You're all that matters to me."

I looked into his eyes. "Dutch, I have to finish it."

"I know, baby. All I'm saying is, when it's over, I'll be here waiting for you. It isn't a matter of seeing how this goes once the mission ends. It's 'I'm here.' Period. Mission or no mission."

I moved off his lap, and he groaned again.

"I have no idea what I want to do with the rest of my life, Dutch."

"I don't care. Whatever it is, we'll make it work."

"What if I don't want anything to do with the intelligence business?"

"I already told you, I'm ready to retire."

"Right," I said. "If I decide to take a teaching position at the University of Virginia, you'll be fine with it."

"If you're serious and you want to live in Charlottesville, there would be a lot I could do."

"You could still work for K19."

"I could, but I don't know if I'd want to. All I'm saying is that whatever you decide you want to do, I'll make it work."

"Why would you do this, Dutch? Why are you pushing so hard?" I stood and wrapped the blanket around me like I had when he came in.

"Don't you feel it?" he said, standing in front of me. "What?"

"The way I feel when I'm with you…I've never…I can't stand the idea of being away from you. Not even for one night. I told Onyx I'd bunk with him tonight to give you space, but I couldn't stay away. I was ready for you to toss me out on my ass again, but I couldn't help it. I had to be with you."

"What if you stop feeling that way?"

"Are you asking me for a commitment, Malin?"

"What if I were?"

Dutch ran his hand through his hair but didn't say anything.

"That's what I thought." I dropped the blanket on the floor. "Just get in bed, Dutch. This is what we know how to do. If it's ever meant to be more, we'll figure it out. In the meantime, I won't ask you to commit anything to me, and you don't ask me to commit anything to you."

"Meaning what? Either of us can just walk away at any time?"

"I'm pretty sure that's how it works when two people are unwilling to commit to each other. I have a long day tomorrow. I need to try to get some sleep."

Dutch crawled into bed next to me. "Malin, I..."

"Don't."

He kissed my cheek. "Okay."


"McTiernan and Copeland should land in about an hour," Doc told us after we'd finished breakfast up at the main house and everyone else left, giving us privacy to talk.

"What happens next?" I asked.

"Once you've met with Ghafor, we hope to have something substantial to dangle in front of Montgomery."

"When will that be?"

"This afternoon."

I couldn't wait, if only to finally know whether the leader of the Islamic State would actually give me the information I so desperately needed.

"Alone?" asked Dutch.

"That's up to Malin," Doc answered.

When I looked up at him, his eyes were guarded, but I knew what he wanted. Dutch wanted me to ask him to be with me, but I couldn't do that. Ghafor had made it clear he'd talk to me and only me. If Dutch were along, he wouldn't say a word.

"Where are we meeting?" I asked.

"Here at the ranch."

"Have you decided where specifically?"

"In the caves," Doc answered. "It'll offer the most privacy as well as the most protection. We can get in there before Monk and Striker deliver Ghafor, and be in position by the time he walks in."

"Meaning what?"

"You aren't going in alone."

I stood from the table and walked toward the front porch. Did they really think a man who lived the life Ghafor did wouldn't sense their presence?

"No," I said, sitting back down. "It won't work."

"Malin—"

"Stay out of this, Dutch," I snapped, more harshly than I'd intended, but this was my mission, mine to finish in the way I believed best. As crucial as the information I needed from Ghafor was, I couldn't risk him refusing to give it to me. That had happened so many times before, I'd lost count.

Doc stared me down, but I refused to give in.

"I'm willing to listen to what you have in mind," he said, surprising me.

"Somewhere out in the vineyard where it's wide open. He'll know you're there, but not close enough to eavesdrop."

"And if he tries—"

I turned my head and looked into Dutch's eyes, silently imploring him to stay out of it.

Dutch stood and walked over to the window. "I don't like it," I heard him mumble.

"It isn't your call, Dutch," Doc responded.

"I know that."

I could see the tension in Dutch's shoulders. The fact that he didn't say anything more told me that he'd respect my wishes. At least, I hoped that's what it meant.

"He won't be armed, and he's requested that you not be either."

Dutch spun around, but I shook my head.

"We'll have her covered," said Doc.

Dutch shook his head, but when his eyes met mine, I knew he was acquiescing, and I couldn't have appreciated it more.

"Thank you," I mouthed.

"If there's nothing else, I'll give you time to prepare." Doc stood and walked out, leaving us alone.

"Mind if we take a walk?" Dutch asked.

"I'd like that."

He took my hand and led me out near the vineyard.

"Thank you," I said again. "I know it's hard for you."

"You have no idea," he said, bringing my hand to his lips. "Fatale gave me a talking to last night."

"Merrigan? What about?"

"She told me a bigger man would know enough to stay out of your way and let you do your job."

"How did that make you feel?"

"Pretty damn small at the time."

When Dutch stopped walking, I stopped too and turned to look at him.

"I want you to know that I don't doubt your abilities as an agent one bit. It isn't about that. It's that I..."

"What, Dutch?"

He ran his hand through his hair and looked out over the vineyard. "You won't believe me."

"Try me."

He cupped my cheek with his palm. "I...want to protect you, Malin."

"Why would you think I wouldn't believe that, Dutch? You've said it often enough."

I smiled and looked into his eyes, wondering what he'd really meant to say but couldn't bring himself to. If it was that he loved me, he was right; I wouldn't have believed him.

I would've told him he was confusing the need to protect me combined with a healthy dose of lust, and maybe even a little regret, with love. He couldn't love me. If he did, he never would've left me without giving it a second thought. I may have forgiven him, but that didn't mean I'd ever risk allowing myself to think Dutch could feel that way about me. I'd done that once, and realizing how wrong I'd been, had nearly destroyed me.

Only having this mission to dive into gave me something else to think about other than how Dutch Miller had ripped my heart from my chest and stomped all over it.

Throwing myself into my work had allowed me to get over him. Or so I'd thought. In the few days we'd been together, I'd found myself slipping too many times. I shook my head at my own stupidity.

"What?"

"Nothing."

"Malin, I—"

"I'm sorry to cut our walk short, but I need to prepare for my meeting with Ghafor." I dropped his hand and walked back in the direction we'd come, praying Dutch wouldn't follow.

I wasn't lying; I did need to prepare. I had to get my mind off the man who'd shared my bed the last few nights, and back on the man who might give me enough information to keep me alive.

# 33

*Dutch*

I'd come so close to telling Malin I loved her, but even to me, the words rang hollow. I did, though, didn't I? Knowing I wanted to be with her from now until the end of time—wasn't that love? Not being able to imagine a day without waking up beside her, hearing the voice that spoke directly to my heart—that had to be love, didn't it?

When Alegria said she only wanted me to be happy, I'd told her that Malin made me feel that way with every breath she took. I hadn't been lying. The words I spoke weren't rehearsed; I had no idea I would say them until I heard them myself.

I watched Malin walk away, wishing I could bring myself to say the words I never believed I'd say again to anyone.

I loved Alegria. I always would, but the way I felt about Malin was so different, so much stronger, more like my life depended on it than what I'd ever felt for the woman I now knew was only ever meant to be my friend.

Last night, Malin had asked how I would've responded if she'd asked me to make a commitment to her while I was in the middle of an op. My response had been knee-jerkingly condescending, but now I knew she was right to get angry. I'd been trying so hard to make sure that she didn't leave me once this was over, I'd lost all sight of how focused she needed to stay until it was.

In a matter of hours, we would know if we had enough to bring down Montgomery and whoever else was involved. If we didn't, Malin would have a target on her back that she might never be able to shake.

Had I considered how terrifying that would be to her? How could she possibly think about a future with me when her own was so uncertain?

What she didn't know was that no matter what happened—if the agency burned her or worse—I'd protect her until my very last breath, as would my K19 partners.

There was time enough for us to talk about what protection she'd need after her meeting with Ghafor. Then we'd know exactly what we were dealing with and could plan the next stage.

I'd started walking back to the house, but stopped and gripped the back of my neck. We wouldn't be planning the next stage of the mission—she would be.

"How are you holding up?" asked Onyx, riding up next to me.

"Terrible. How was your ride?" I looked up at the horse my friend was on. "What the hell is that, a draft horse?"

"Yeah," Onyx chuckled. "Ol' Huck belongs to Naughton. He thought I might like to take him out when he saw the ride Alex's brothers brought for me."

I laughed too. Montano "Onyx" Yáñez had to weigh in at three hundred pounds at least, all of which was solid muscle. A lesser horse might collapse under him.

Onyx dismounted and walked alongside me. "What's the plan for today?"

"Malin will be meeting Ghafor out here," I answered, making a sweeping motion with my arm.

"Seriously?"

I rolled my eyes. *"Seriously, bro."*

"When are we being briefed?"

"I don't know."

Onyx took out his phone, probably to text Doc. He didn't bother putting it back in his pocket while he waited for a response.

"Eleven hundred," he said after his phone vibrated and he read what was on the screen.

"Roger that."

"I'll catch you later, bro," he said, getting back on the horse.

I waved as my friend rode away. I had a hell of a lot of thinking to do.

# 34

*Malin*

It would be interesting to see whether Ghafor was his usual cocky self this afternoon or if the fact that he'd been taken down a few notches would bring his ego into check. Doubtful, especially with me, which was probably why he'd demanded that he only talk to me, and that it had to be alone. He believed he could intimidate me.

He couldn't be more wrong. Something had changed inside of me the day Orlov held a gun to my head and Dutch had shot him.

The first thing I'd wanted to do was kill Dutch for taking out one of the two people I'd come to desperately need. The second thing I'd felt was relief. In that moment, I'd known I was no longer alone.

I'd fought it so hard, but the truth was, knowing Dutch was with me gave me the courage I needed to see this through. It wouldn't matter what Ghafor told me— even if it wasn't anything I could use to bring down Montgomery.

I heard the door to the cottage open, and I stood.

"Hey," Dutch said, coming around the corner. "If you need me to go back out, I can."

I walked over and put my arms around his neck. "That's the last thing I want."

Dutch put his hands on my hips and brought my body closer to his. "You sure about that?"

I reached up and kissed him. "More than I've been sure of anything in a long time."

He took my hands from around his neck. "Believe me, there is nothing I'd like more than to sweep you off your feet, carry you upstairs, and find out exactly how sure you are, but, baby, I gotta ask where this is coming from. Not less than an hour ago, you needed to be alone. Now—"

I rested two fingers on his lips and then put my arms back around his neck. "That's just it. I'm not alone. For the first time in over a year, I'm not, and I have you to thank for that."

"What's changed, Malin?" He moved my arms again and walked far enough away that I couldn't touch him.

"I was thinking about meeting with Ghafor, and it dawned on me that I wasn't afraid. Whatever happens, I know I'm not alone. I know that even if I don't get what we need to bring Montgomery down, that won't be the end. You'll help me figure out what I need to do next."

"I thought that was exactly what you didn't want."

"It wasn't, or that's what I told myself. Until I realized what was behind my bravado, and that's you."

"You could handle this all on your own, baby. In fact, you did."

"And the whole time I second-guessed myself. I let Ghafor push me around. I let him demand I hand you over to Safi. I let him force me to kidnap Alegria. I let him. I didn't stand up to him, because I was afraid."

Dutch shook his head. "No. You did what you knew you needed to do."

"I don't want to argue with you. What I want you to know is that I'm done pushing you out of my way when I know damn well that you're the reason I'm here to begin with."

"Tell me what you want me to do."

"I haven't figured that out yet."

"Fair enough. How much time have you got?"

"Give or take three hours."

"Let's get at it, then."

"Ready?" Dutch asked three hours later.

"I am, how about you?"

"Sure enough."

Together, we'd decided that Abdul Ghafor no longer called the shots and we needed to stop treating him like he did. I would meet with him, but it wouldn't be out in a damn vineyard. It would be inside the winery where Dutch and Doc would be close, along with as many others of the K19 team I decided I wanted to be visible.

Ghafor wasn't armed, because that same team had taken away his weapons. There was no reason why any of us needed to be armed.

"We need to brief Doc."

"You're sure he'll go along with it?"

Dutch laughed. "Oh, yeah. He's probably struggling as much as I am to stay out of it."

When we walked into the winery, I saw that Razor, Gunner, and Onyx were waiting with Doc.

"Ranger, Diesel, and Striker will be on their way as soon as we give the word," said Doc.

I nodded, looking around the room. "Thank you all for being here."

"Tell us what you want us to do, Starling," said Gunner, winking.

I felt Dutch stiffen behind me and looked over my shoulder. "Consider the source," I muttered. "Thank you, Gunner." I looked him in the eye and saw respect mirrored back at me.

I outlined everything Dutch and I had discussed. "The plan is to get Ghafor to agree to testify in exchange for exile, if that's what he's looking for. If he wants to return to the Middle East, we'll make that happen instead."

"The one thing we haven't talked about is what state his organization is in presently," said Doc.

"He's kidnapping former CIA agents, asking for hundred-million-dollar ransoms, and recruiting women as soldiers for Allah."

"He's done," said Gunner.

I agreed. "He won't choose to go back."

"Rumors of his demise, then, aren't premature."

I nodded, feeling as though Gunner was reading my mind.

"Where are we stashing him?" he asked Doc.

"We'll find a place where it's hotter than hell most of the year."

"South America somewhere," said Razor, looking at something on his laptop. "McTiernan says Montgomery is headed in to see him," he added, raising his head.

"We ready?" asked Doc.

"We are," I answered, looking at Dutch, who nodded.

"Let's get him here."

"How far out is he?" asked Onyx.

"He's at the Harmony safe house, which gives us about thirty minutes." Doc turned from him to me. "You have time to rework this if you've changed your mind about any part of it."

"There's nothing I want to change."

Doc nodded. "Let's move," he said to the rest of the men in the room.

"Where's Merrigan?" I asked once only Dutch, Doc, and I were left.

"Back in Montecito along with my parents, where they'll stay until this is finished."

# 35

*Dutch*

Malin's question and Doc's answer reminded me that this wasn't the dangerous part of the mission. That would come later, as soon as we fed Deputy Director Montgomery enough to get him to act. Before he left, McTiernan assured them that from everything he'd learned, the man would work alone. I didn't have enough confidence in Kellen to believe he knew one way or another.

"You're quiet," she said when Doc excused himself.

I nodded.

"Everything okay?"

"No. It isn't."

When Malin's brow furrowed, I smoothed the creases with my finger. "Tell me you're sure this is the way you want this to go down."

"I've told you over and over again that it is."

"I don't want you to look back at this and feel as though you were pressured into handling it in a way you hadn't originally intended to."

"I'm sure what we're doing is right, Dutch. Why are you second-guessing me now?"

I walked her backwards until her back was up against the stone wall of the room and grasped the back of her neck. I brought my forehead to hers and closed my eyes, knowing that this wasn't the time to tell her how I felt—that I loved her more than I'd known I was capable of. To do so would not only be selfish, it would be dangerous. Instead, I kissed her, thrusting my tongue into her mouth while I held her still, forcing her to take what I gave. I couldn't tell her with words, but this way I could.

"What is this about, Dutch?" she asked, pulling back to look in my eyes.

I couldn't answer. If I spoke, I'd say everything I knew I shouldn't. When I tried to pull away, she grabbed me.

"Don't walk away from me," she pleaded. "Talk to me."

I shook my head. "I'm protecting you."

"What does that really mean, Dutch?"

"You know what it means."

"Tell me."

"I can't. Not now."

"Yes, now. Please."

I closed my eyes and looked up at the ceiling. "Malin…"

"Tell me, Dutch," she whispered.

I looked into her eyes and cupped her cheek with my palm. "I love you, Malin. I hope you know how much."

Her eyes filled with tears. "I love you, Dutch."

I studied her, wanting to ask a thousand questions, but none more than why she'd let me tell her now. With everything she had in front of her, why now? But I didn't. Instead, I kissed her, letting my mouth and tongue tell her again how I felt.

# 36

*Malin*

As hard as it was to do, I pulled away from Dutch when I heard people entering the winery.

"They're through the gate," said Razor.

I sat at the table in the middle of the room and grasped Dutch's hand when he sat beside me.

"I'll be right over there," he said, motioning with his head to the place we'd agreed he'd be positioned. "You've got this, baby."

I nodded. "I do."

Doc moved from where he stood talking to Gunner to his assigned spot.

I would be the only one who spoke to Ghafor, but the man would know that I had backup close enough to act or even intervene if necessary.

I heard the heavy door open and raised my head, looking directly into the man's eyes.

"This is not what we agreed," he said to Striker as they walked toward me.

"Special Agent Kilbourne made the rules," he responded.

Ghafor's eyes never left mine, and I didn't blink.

"Let's get right to it," I said when he was seated.

Ghafor nodded.

"What did United Russia pay you to do?"

He smiled. "If you know United Russia was behind it, you don't need any further information from me. You already have your answers."

"I want to hear it from you. In detail."

Ghafor looked around the room at the men I now considered my team. He had two choices. He could answer me, or he could face whatever his imagination had conjured up they'd do to him.

"Before we begin." I placed a recording device in front of him and turned it on. "Go ahead."

Ghafor leaned back in his chair. "Also, before I begin…"

"No, Abdul. Let's see what you have for us before we promise to give you anything."

# 37

*Dutch*

"Think it's enough?" I asked Striker while Ranger and Diesel led Ghafor out of the winery and back into the SUV that would return him to the safe house.

"It's more than I thought we'd have."

"She's good," I said, looking over at Malin.

"She's okay," answered Striker, walking away.

Malin was head-to-head with Doc, playing back everything Ghafor had said. In the end, we'd agreed to give him the protection he needed in exchange for his testimony before Congress—if it came to that. With everything he'd told Malin, I could already see the heads rolling down Pennsylvania Avenue, beginning with the man now considered the leader of the free world.

When Doc left, I walked over to her.

"Good job, Malin."

She smiled up at me. "The best part is that he gave us the proof Orlov would've." She closed her eyes briefly and then opened them and looked into mine. "I'm sorry, I didn't mean—"

I put my fingers on her lips. "Shh. I know you didn't."

When she smiled again, I wanted to lift her up and spin her in the air, but we weren't alone. Instead, I leaned in as close to her as I could get.

"Do you have any idea how proud I am of you?"

"You are?"

"Damn right, I am."

"Thank you for making me realize I needed your help."

"You didn't, but I'll let you thank me anyway. Later, though."

She kissed me.

"We have work to do, Starling," we both heard Gunner say as he walked up to the table.

"Stage two begins now."

"Give her a minute to revel in her glory," said Razor, walking up beside him. "Okay, minute's up. Dutch, remove your hands from Special Agent Kilbourne so she can brief us on what she wants us to do next."

Malin laughed and rolled her eyes. "You're pretty good for my ego. I am a junior agent, you know."

"Junior agent?" said Gunner. "I thought you were coming on board as a partner."

Malin looked at me, and I shook my head. "I didn't suggest to anyone that you wanted to join K19."

"Why the hell not?" asked Gunner.

"I'll let Malin speak for herself."

All eyes turned to her.

"Now probably wouldn't be a good time for you to put her on the spot," I added.

"I repeat, why the hell not?" Gunner walked over to Malin so he was close enough that I could see she was uncomfortable. "This is one of the biggest ops I've ever seen in my career," he said to her. "Stay with the agency if you want to, but you can do a lot more good in the world if you don't have your hands tied all the time."

"I'm not sure I want to stay in intelligence."

I was prepared to intervene if Gunner kept up his confrontation, but he didn't. Instead, he shook his head, walked to the other side of the table, and took a seat.

"Let's get to work," said Razor, sitting next to Gunner. "Out of everything Ghafor told you, which part do you think will make Montgomery act?"

# 38

*Malin*

After an hour of hashing it out, I was convinced we knew exactly what we needed to do.

"If McTiernan tells Montgomery I have evidence substantial enough that once the attorney general hears it, he'll appoint a special prosecutor, it'll be enough."

"What about McTiernan?" asked Dutch.

"Going off the grid, at least as far as Monty's access to him. He's being pulled for an NSA mission. Copeland is out too," said Razor.

"Not a lie," added Gunner, chuckling. "That oughta make Monty crap his britches."

"If there isn't anything else for us to discuss…" I looked at each of the men in the room, all of whom seemed surprised that I was ready to end the meeting. "I'd like to make some notes."

Gunner nodded and motioned for Razor to follow him.

"What do you need, Malin?" Dutch asked when we were alone.

"A break." I walked into his arms and rested my head on his chest. "I know you guys probably think I'm a wimp, but I need time to think."

Dutch laughed. "There isn't a person who's met you who thinks you're a wimp."

I took Dutch's hand and led him out of the winery and to the walkway that led to the cottage.

"What's goin' on, baby?" he asked when I walked up the stairs as soon as we were inside.

"If you follow me, you'll find out."

I laughed when Dutch took the stairs two at a time to catch up. I walked straight into the bathroom and up to the bath's control panel.

"I'm sure I could figure this out, but I think it would be quicker if you pushed whatever buttons fill the tub."

"My pleasure," he said, putting his hands on my shoulders and shifting me out of his way.

I shed my clothes and stepped into the warm swirling water. When Dutch did the same and settled behind me. I relaxed into him.

"Mmm, I really needed this," I moaned when he kneaded the muscles in my shoulders.

"You're pretty tightly wound, baby."

"How long do you think it will be before we hear something about Montgomery?"

Dutch kissed my neck right below my ear. "Long enough that we don't need to think about it right now." He ran the tip of his tongue down to my shoulder and moved his hands down the front of my body.

When I tried to move, he held me in place.

"Let me do this," he said, trapping my arms under his.

"Dutch?"

"Mm-hmm?"

"Did you mean it?"

"I never would've said it if I didn't, Malin."

"Say it again."

"I love you."

"I love you too."

I felt his hardness twitch behind me and wiggled my bottom.

"You feel what hearing you tell me you love me did to me?"

"I do."

Dutch moved his hand under my arm and cupped my pussy. "Does it do the same thing to you, baby?"

"You know it does."

I shifted away from him, stood, and turned around so I could straddle his thighs.

"I need you." I guided him inside me. This would be the first time our bodies would join together since we both said "I love you." Would it feel different between us?

Wrapping my arms around his neck and crushing my breasts against his chest, I waited until I couldn't keep still another second. When I started to move, Dutch grabbed my hips, making me adjust to his rhythm.

My fingernails dug into the skin on his back when he increased the pace of his thrusts and his breathing changed.

I put my hands on the side of his face, meeting his gaze.

"I love you," I told him when I felt like my eyes would roll back in my head from the pleasure radiating from my core out as far as my fingers and toes.

Dutch thrust one more time. "Look at me," he groaned as my eyes drifted closed. "I love you, Malin."

I could feel him pulsing inside me.

"We aren't finished," he told me when we both stood in the tub. "Wait for me on the bed." He wrapped one of the warm plush around me.

He dropped his towel and lay on the bed, next to me. Chill bumps covered my naked body as he ran his fingers over my skin.

"We need to talk, Malin."

I opened my eyes and looked into his.

"I know the timing is terrible, but I can't stand not knowing if you feel the same way I do."

I reached up and cupped his cheek with my hand. "I do, Dutch. I told you I love you."

"I need more than that. When this thing is over, I need to know that you and I are going to be together. It doesn't matter to me if you want to leave the business; I told you we'll figure it out."

I moved my hand from his cheek to behind his neck and pulled him close enough that I could join my mouth with his. I kissed him, pushing my tongue through his lips. He kissed me back, but then pulled away.

"Yes, Dutch," I said, looking into his eyes. "We'll figure it out."

"That's all I needed to know."

# 39

*Dutch*

I checked my phone repeatedly, but there was no update from anyone regarding Montgomery or McTiernan. Malin hadn't heard anything either.

While I didn't mind the time alone with her, I knew the stress of not hearing was eating away at her as much as it was me.

I'd declined the invitation to join the group for dinner at the main house. Instead, Malin and I made dinner from what we could find in the cottage. As if by magic, all the fixings for spaghetti and meatballs had appeared in the refrigerator.

"Are we pretending again?" she asked when she set the bowl of pasta in front of me.

"I'm not. Are you?"

She shook her head. "Will it last, Dutch?"

"Once this is over?"

Malin nodded.

"It will."

"How can you be certain?"

"I can't accept anything else, Malin." I stood and held my hand out to her. "Come here." I pulled her onto my lap and nuzzled her neck. "I know you feel like we're in limbo, and as far as the rest of the world goes, we are. But between you and me, we aren't waiting for anything to happen or anything to change, except maybe where we're living. Otherwise, this is us, baby."

As if on cue to spoil the moment between us, my phone buzzed at the same time Malin's did.

She didn't move, so I pulled mine out, punched in my access code, and let her see the screen.

"He's on the move," she said and I nodded. When it pinged again, she looked at the screen a second time. "McTiernan has his flight plan, although it's filed under an assumed name, of course."

"Is he flying alone?"

Malin typed the question on the screen and hit send.

"Affirmative," she answered a few moments later.

"He believes he can handle this."

After taking a deep breath, Malin nodded and stood, setting my phone on the table.

"Tell me what you're thinking," I said.

"I expect fixers will come from every direction."

I nodded. "Although Montgomery has too much of an ego to believe any of them can handle you as well as he can."

"He comes from an era where there weren't fixers, at least not officially known as such."

"We'll be ready, no matter how many they send."

"Doc wants us to meet him in the winery," she said, holding up her phone.

"After we eat."

For a moment, I thought Malin might protest, but she picked up her fork instead.

"You know what amazes me?"

She raised her head.

"It doesn't matter what ingredients you have to work with, the sauce and meatballs always taste the same."

She laughed and shook her head. "No, they don't."

I scrunched my eyes. "They do to me."

"You're silly."

"Wanna know why?"

"Okay. I'll bite. Why, Dutch?"

"Cuz it always tastes like you made it just for me. Just because you know how much I love it, and since you love me, that's all I taste."

She shook her head again. "I'm not sure I follow that, but as long as you're happy, that's all that matters."

"You make me happy with every breath you take, baby."

Her cheeks along with that sweet spot on her neck turned pink, making me wish that, instead of going to meet Doc, I could carry her upstairs and ravage all the anxiety out of her body so all she could feel was me.

"You make me happy too, Dutch."

"Ready?"

"Not really."

"Let's finish this, Malin, so we can get on with the rest of our lives."

# 40

*Malin*

While the danger I faced now was less than I had many times during this mission, the nervousness I felt was twice as intense. This was it. One way or another, by this time tomorrow, the last vestiges of the work I'd done for the past year would come to a culmination.

What would it feel like to wake up in a few days and know this was all behind me? The mission I'd accepted to give myself time to get over Dutch, at least in part, had become the very thing that brought him back into my life.

Now here we were, not just working together, but loving each other too.

"Let's go," said Dutch, holding his hand out to me.

I picked up the angel ornament that sat on the table and twirled it on my finger. "I'm tempted to bring it with me. Is that silly?"

"Not at all. Put it in your pocket, baby."

I smiled and followed his suggestion.

"Let's run through this one more time," Doc said when Dutch and I walked into the winery. "Montgomery's plane will land in under an hour. He knows how to make contact with Malin. What we anticipate is that he'll make nice and ask for a meeting so she can brief him on the outcome of the mission he believes she's ready to wrap."

I felt myself wanting to chew my fingernails, a habit I'd broken in high school. All of our plans were predicated on Montgomery doing exactly as Doc had just laid out. If he didn't, we'd have to adjust on the fly.

I watched Dutch pace, aware that his anxiety was greater than my own, just like it would be for me if he was about to put himself in the direct path of danger.

Several of the K19 team were already staked out in various places in the winery, although even I had no idea where they were. The plan was that I would suggest Montgomery meet me there.

Once we heard from him, Gunner and Razor would be out front, while Dutch was in the back. Doc would be closest to me.

Dutch didn't liked it, but between the two of us, Doc and I had convinced him that neither Doc nor the other four men positioned in the winery would let anything happen to me. Above all else, I was armed and perfectly capable of defending myself.

"He's thirty minutes out," Doc relayed from the radio headset. I held my breath. What was Montgomery waiting for?

As if on cue, my cell phone vibrated. "Kilbourne," I answered.

"Agent Kilbourne, you've been one difficult woman to track down."

"Yes, sir."

"McTiernan briefed me on your mission. I understand you've uncovered something quite significant."

I tapped my lip, waiting for him to get to the point. "Yes, sir," I said a second time.

"Director Flatley has sent me to do a full debrief as well as to offer his congratulations for a job well done."

"Where, sir?"

"I've just arrived in San Luis Obispo and am heading your way. Is now a good time for us to meet?"

"This is unexpected. When will you be arriving?"

"In less than a half hour."

"That soon?" I asked, giving Doc a thumbs-up. "I mean, of course, sir."

"I'd rather not disrupt the Butler Family. Is there a place where we can meet privately?"

I ended the call after assuring Montgomery that the outer gate to the ranch would be left open, and that I'd be waiting in the winery.

"Showtime," said Razor, grasping Gunner's shoulder. "Let's move out."

Dutch walked over and put his arms around my waist. "I'm sorry to do this with an audience, but I have to." He bent down and kissed me. "I love you," he whispered.

"I love you," I whispered back.

Dutch groaned and looked up at the ceiling. "I have to go, as much as I don't want to."

"I'll come with you," I told him, looking back at Doc. "Potty break."

I blew Dutch a kiss before going in the door to the ladies' bathroom.

I felt on the wall for the light switch, flicked it a couple of times, but it didn't go on. Just as I turned to go back out, I felt someone's arm encircle my waist. The man's opposite hand covered my mouth. Before I could utter a sound, darkness engulfed me.

# 41

*Dutch*

I was crouched just outside the winery's door, by the loading dock, when I thought I heard a noise from inside. I drew my gun and was about to run in when something heavy hit my head, and everything went black.

"What the fuck?" I heard a familiar voice shout through the haze in my addled brain.

"Dutch!" the voice yelled, and I opened my eyes. "Where's Malin?"

"What do you mean? She went into the bathroom." I sat up, my body shaky as I looked at Doc, who was shouting orders I couldn't understand through the mic on his headset.

"Can you stand?" Doc asked, pulling me up.

Barely, but I wouldn't tell him that. "I'm getting fucking tired of people hitting me over the head." Once on my feet, the haziness in my brain dissipated as Doc's words sunk in.

"You asked me where Malin was. What the hell happened?"

"She didn't come back," Doc muttered while listening to what someone was saying through the headset.

"What do you mean she didn't come back?" I yelled, grasping my throbbing head.

"Roger that," said Doc into the mic before putting his hand on my shoulder. "Can you handle a gun?"

"Of course I can handle a fucking gun," I shouted, feeling for it. When I didn't find it, I grabbed the one Doc held out to me. "Where is she?"

"Caves."

I felt adrenaline surge through my veins as I followed Doc through the darkness to the wine caves. I knew better than to ask what had happened. Now my focus had to stay on Doc's movements as we stealthily made our way to the entrance.

"Montgomery?" I whispered when we met Gunner and Razor near the heavy gate.

Doc shook his head. "Decoy. Hang on," he said, focusing on the words coming through the headset.

"Roger that," he responded, motioning us away from the entrance. "Burns has them live," he said, pulling a piece of paper out of his back pocket.

I watched Doc draw a line representing the cave's entrance and then several offshoots.

"You can't tell when you go in, but if you go far enough, there's an outer ring that connects all the rooms. They're here." Doc pointed to the first hallway on the right, and then to the first storage room.

"Who's got her?" I growled, my hand gripping the gun until my knuckles were white.

"Flatley."

# 42

*Malin*

I straightened my stiff neck and opened my eyes. I looked down at the ropes binding my body to a chair and then up at the man sitting in front of me.

"Kilbourne," he said.

I couldn't decide how to address the man speaking to me. Certainly not as Director Flatley. I wouldn't show him the respect that the Director of the Central Intelligence Agency normally warranted. I'd rather spit at him. Instead, I remained silent.

"You already know how this will go. You'll tell me everything I need to know, and I'll spare the life of your friend over there."

I turned my head and looked at the body slumped and tied to a chair like I was. Flatley walked over, grabbed the hair of the unconscious woman, and yanked her head up so I could see Sofia's face.

He dropped her head and stalked back over to where I sat.

I nodded.

"Let's start with Abdul Ghafor."

I glanced over when I heard Sofia groan.

Flatley heard it too and was about to hit the woman with the butt of his gun when I screamed at him to stop.

The man stood where he was and waited.

"He was paid to direct terrorist cells across the country to hack into the electronic vote tabulation during the last election, along with the optical scanners that tabulate mail-in ballots."

"Where did the money come from?"

"A Super PAC."

"Where originally?"

"Why are you—" I stopped talking when I saw Flatley pull back his arm as though he was going to strike Sofia.

"I ask the questions. Where did the money come from?"

"I don't know."

I cried out but was too late to stop him from hitting Sofia so hard the chair fell on its side with her in it.

"That's what happens when you lie to me. Where did the money come from?"

"United Russia."

"Keep talking."

Afraid that if Flatley hit Sofia again, she might not be able to withstand the injury he'd cause, I continued.

"What else do you want to know?"

"What did United Russia get in exchange for their money?"

"The president pushed the Treasury to let UR convert $5.7 billion of funds held in an offshore account from dollars into rubles."

Flatley paced back and forth in front of me. "What kind of proof do you have that any of this really happened, Special Agent Kilbourne?"

"I don't."

He stopped and studied me.

"Who does?"

"The attorney general."

Flatley smiled.

I blinked but didn't dare close my eyes. Right there, that was the proof I'd needed. The only question left unanswered had been whether the president's two-term attorney general was in on it.

Flatley pulled out his phone. "We're done here," I heard him say.

# 43

*Dutch*

"He got it," said Doc.

"All of it?" I asked.

"Every word."

"Who's in there?"

"Malin, Flatley, and an unnamed woman. My guess is that it may be Descanso."

"Where's Onyx?"

"Westside. Why?"

"Descanso."

Doc nodded.

While Doc's father had continued to monitor the conversation between Flatley and Malin, Doc had drawn out a map of who would go in where.

Burns Butler wasn't just a technological wizard who had wired every corner of the wine caves both for audio and visual monitoring, the construction had taken three times as long as had originally been quoted since he'd insisted on several entrances and exits to be worked into the design.

"You're sure Flatley doesn't have any backup?" asked Razor.

Doc repeated his question through the mic.

"Burns reports there is no other activity inside the caves. However, Flatley may have someone on the outside who he just made contact with."

"On it," said Gunner, moving out with Razor. To where, I didn't know.

"You got this, Dutch?"

"Yes, sir."

"Look at me."

Doc tracked my eye movement. "I'll lead. You follow. Understood."

"Understood."

"Let's move," Doc said through the mic and then turned to me. "We're closest."

I nodded, following Doc as he made his way through the caves, keeping my body up against the stone walls.

I froze momentarily when I heard a man's voice telling Malin to move. Doc made eye contact, and I nodded again, quickly moving to the other side of the corridor, but still out of view.

When Doc signaled, we turned into the room simultaneously.

"Freeze and lower your weapon," Doc shouted at the second man I had witnessed holding a gun to Malin's head.

Like with Orlov, I studied the look on Malin's face. Then, I'd seen fear, but it wasn't of Orlov. It was of K19 destroying her mission. Now I knew the difference.

This time Malin was afraid of the man holding her hostage. I lowered my chin, just slightly, and at the same moment saw Malin mimic my movement, I fired, and Flatley fell to the ground.

I ran toward Malin as the K19 team filed into the room. Time stopped for me as we clung to each other amid the chaos.

"Sofia—" Malin cried.

"Onyx has her," said Doc. "They'll transport her to the hospital via helicopter."

"Will she be okay?"

Doc nodded. "It looks like what he did was more for show than to inflict any real injury."

I held Malin tight in my arms. The noise in the background fell away as I listened to her breathe. I put my hand on her heart and closed my eyes, concentrating on its rhythmic beat.

She did the same with me, one hand on my heart while the other cupped my cheek. Our foreheads rested against one another. "You're hurt," she said, touching the dried blood in my hair.

I smiled. "Nothing out of the ordinary. I seem to get hit over the head a lot. Better than being shot."

Doc walked over to us and put a hand on each of our shoulders. "We're clear," he said. "Gunner and Razor have Montgomery secured."

"He was here?" I asked, tearing my eyes away from Malin's beautiful face. "I thought he was the decoy?"

Doc nodded. "He was, along with Flatley's transport."

"Is he dead?" asked Malin.

I spoke before Doc could. "Let's get you out of here."

As we rounded the corner, I saw the CIA director's body on a stretcher, covered with a blanket.

Malin gasped.

"I'm sorry," I said, leading her past him and out the main entrance of the cave.

Once outside, she stopped. "Dutch, wait."

I rolled my shoulders, not wanting to hear what I knew she was going to say.

Malin looked into my eyes. "I'm glad he's dead, Dutch."

"You are?"

"I don't care if I have to go into the witness protection program, or live my life in outer Mongolia. I'm done with this whole thing. Even the attorney general is in on it. What they did is reprehensible, but I still can't prove it. It's time for me to let it go."

"No, it isn't. Burns recorded the whole thing."

"Flatley didn't say a word. I did all the talking."

"Montgomery doesn't know that."

"Do you think he'll confess?"

"I do. That, combined with Ghafor's statement, and I feel confident heads are going to roll." I laughed out loud.

"Why are you laughing?"

I put my arm around her shoulders, and we kept walking. "I'm sorry, but earlier—it may have been yesterday or even the day before—I pictured the president's head rolling down Pennsylvania Avenue."

"It would be what he deserves. What happens next? I mean, I know he can be impeached and even prosecuted, but does the vice president get sworn in even though there's proof that the election results were fraudulent?"

"I have no idea, but I bet I know who would."

"Who, Burns?"

"Exactly."

# 44

*Malin*

"Sofia's going to be fine," Onyx reassured me when he called to say he'd be spending the night with her at the hospital. "Flatley roughed her up a little, but she doesn't have any broken bones, just a minor concussion."

"Please tell her how sorry I am."

I heard muffled sounds on the phone and then voices in the background.

"Sofia said there's nothing for you to be sorry for."

"Can I come see her?"

"She'll be out of the hospital tomorrow, and I'm taking her straight home."

"Back to South Carolina?"

"Yes, ma'am."

"That sounds so nice."

"I'd be willing to bet that Dutch would jump at the chance to take you back there too."

I smiled. "Good night, Onyx. Take care of Miss Sofia, okay?"

"What was that all about?" Dutch asked when I came to sit next to him.

"Onyx is taking Sofia back to South Carolina tomorrow."

He groaned. "God, I envy them."

"How soon do you think we'll be able to leave?"

Dutch smiled. "For South Carolina?"

I nodded.

"I'm ready to go right now."

"Hold on there," said Doc. "First, Malin has to wrap this mission."

"Can't someone else do it?"

I slugged Dutch's arm. "And have them take credit for all my hard work?"

"Ouch." Dutch rubbed the spot where I hit him. "I was thinking more along the lines of delegating it to someone."

"I'm a junior agent, Dutch. No one works under me."

"About that," said Doc.

Both Dutch and I shook our heads.

"I'm taking leave, and Malin is not open for discussion about her future employment, whatever that may be."

"Taking leave?" said Doc, laughing. "You're long since out of the military, boy."

"I'll resign, then."

"The hell you will."

"Come on, Doc. Give me a break. I'm not kidding when I say I need some time away."

Doc put his hand on Dutch's shoulder. "Merrigan already told me she'll refuse to put you on any schedule for at least six months. After that, it's at your discretion."

"Are we going to have anyone who's actually working left?" asked Razor, walking in with Gunner.

"Who's in the active column?" asked Dutch.

"Striker and Monk. I don't know about Mantis and Alegria," answered Doc.

"We need to rethink this partner policy," said Gunner. "Every time we make someone a partner, six months later, they want to retire. Maybe we should consider adding a few employees."

"Merrigan said the same thing."

"Smart woman."

"Hey, Gunner, are you gonna tell them, or am I?"

"What's that, Raze?"

"Montgomery."

"Right. That *sonuvabitch* was ready to confess everything before we even got him in the car."

"Malin asked what happens next, and I told her I had no idea."

Doc rubbed the back of his neck. "Jesus, I guess it'll be up to the Supreme Court to decide. There certainly isn't a precedent."

"There are no political recall mechanisms available to voters at the federal level at all," said Razor. "Not even congressionally."

"What if the vice president was in on it?"

"If he's impeached and kicked out of office, the speaker of the house becomes president."

"Did Montgomery name names?" I asked.

"Oh, yeah," answered Razor. "Got 'em all right here." He held up his phone.

"Is that legal?" asked Dutch.

Razor laughed. "Hell, no."

"Was the vice president's name mentioned?" I asked.

"Nah, but who knows what will come out when he gives his official testimony."

My phone vibrated, and I pulled it out of my pocket. "Kilbourne," I answered without looking at the screen.

"Hey, Malin. It's Sumner."

I got up and walked away from the group. "Hey, Cope. What can I do for you?"

"I just want you to know, McTiernan and I really did have your back even though we couldn't make you aware of it at the time."

"I appreciate it. Was there another reason you called?"

"Yeah, he wanted me to tell you that you're on eight weeks administrative leave."

"What?" I gasped. "Why?"

"Settle down, Kilbourne. This is a good thing. One, it's paid leave. Two, you've earned it. And three, there are going to be some major shakeups at the agency in the coming weeks."

"I guess that makes sense. Although I do have a report to write."

"Turn it in and then forget about it. We'll take it from there, and before you say anything, this was your mission, no one else's. We were backup, even McTiernan said so."

I thanked him and ended the call. Did it really matter who got credit? It wasn't as though I planned to stay at the agency anyway, even if they still wanted me to.

I looked over at Dutch, laughing and surrounded by people who cared about him. Whether I returned to the CIA or not, I'd never have the kind of relationships the K19 team did with one another. It wasn't limited to the guys either. Merrigan and Alegria were a part of the camaraderie.

Dutch walked over to where I stood off to the side. "What are you thinking about, baby?" he asked, stroking my cheek with his finger.

"I'm embarrassed to admit it, but I'm jealous of the relationship you have with your team and that all of you have with one another."

"You're part of it whether you want to be or not. I bet if you asked any one of those guys, they'd say, as far as they're concerned, you're already one of us."

"How would you feel about that?"

"Working with you?"

I nodded.

"Hey, Doc, do we have any rules about partner fraternization?"

"If we do, Merrigan's going to have to fire me."

"So, no?"

"Hell, no," Doc answered, shaking his head.

"Then, it's all good as far as I'm concerned. There's no way in hell I could go back to having to keep my hands off you."

"I'm not saying I'm committed to anything at this point."

"Nothing at all?" he asked, pushing his lower lip out.

"Oh my God. Are you whining?"

"I'm so whining right now."

"I'm not committed to anything professionally."

"What about personally?"

"Are you asking me for a commitment, Dutch?"

"Damn straight."

"What are you willing to do in return?"

"Add your name to the deed on Cokabow Island."

I laughed. "You're joking."

"I'm not, although I do have one condition."

"What's that?"

Dutch wrapped his arms around my waist and pulled me in as close as I could get. He leaned down and nipped at my earlobe. "Let's get out of here," he whispered.

"Lead the way."

# 45

*Dutch*

"Good night," I hollered, taking Malin's hand and leading her out of the winery and over to the cottage. I didn't bother to wait to see if anyone heard me or not.

"This doesn't feel right," I said before I opened the door to go inside.

"No?"

I shook my head. "Come with me." I put my arm around Malin's shoulders and led her over to the swing on the porch of the main house. When I sat down, I pulled her onto my lap. "This is better."

"I like this too."

I cupped her cheek with my palm. "Look at me. I want you to know I was serious back there."

"Dutch, it's okay. We have plenty of time to figure things out."

"I don't need time. I love you, Malin, and I want to spend the rest of my life with you. I'm not joking about the island. I told you that I already talked to Doc, Gunner, and Razor about it. They're more than willing to sell it to me."

"What's your one condition?"

"When I add your name to the deed, I want it to be Malin Kilbourne-Miller."

"Dutch, are you asking—"

"Yes, I'm asking you to marry me. I know my timing sucks, and when you tell our kids about the way I proposed, they're going to think I'm the least romantic guy that ever lived, but I can't wait another minute. Marry me, Malin."

"Yes, Dutch, I'll marry you, and when I tell our kids the story of how you proposed, I'll say it was under the light of the moon, on a porch swing that looked out over a beautiful vineyard, and they'll think you're the *most* romantic guy that ever lived."

# Epilogue

### *Dutch*

"I really need to run, Dutch," Malin said, trying to coax me out of bed. Instead, I pulled her back in.

"Not yet."

"But it's—"

"If you're about to tell me what time it is, I'll remind you, we're on the island, which means we don't live by a clock."

"It'll be too hot if we wait."

"Then, we'll run later, after it cools down."

Malin folded her arms.

"Are you pouting?"

"I am so pouting."

"Okay, okay. I'll get up."

When Malin smiled and scooted out of my arms, a warmth settled in my chest.

The last three months had been heaven. Malin had turned in her report and did exactly as McTiernan and Copeland wanted her to—she stopped thinking about it.

The only hiccup had been with Ghafor, who had insisted he be given exile in Buenaventura, Colombia.

I'd managed to keep Malin out of it, at her request, but when Striker got wind of where Ghafor wanted to go, he fought it as hard as he could.

In the end, McTiernan, along with the state department, overruled him. That hadn't been an easy pill for the man who had once had McTiernan's job to swallow.

Otherwise, there had been fourteen indictments, beginning with Ed Montgomery and going straight up the chain of command. The prediction was, there would be several more. The president's impeachment hearings would begin in the next couple of weeks, and as far as anyone could tell, the vice president had been completely unaware of the president's actions.

I was glad. He seemed like a good guy, although knowing who the good and bad guys were, wasn't always an easy thing to do.

Malin and I had gone to the courthouse in Charleston the day after Doc told us to get the hell out of California, and got married. Neither of us had cared about any kind of fanfare, including having anyone stand up with us.

Malin had been worried I'd be disappointed about not having Mantis and Alegria there, but as I told her, the truth was, I didn't want them at our wedding.

"This is us," I'd told her. "You and me. We're all that matters."

Merrigan had called once, asking if Malin would be interested in joining K19, but she told her she wasn't ready to make any decision about her professional future.

For now, our only commitments were to each other and growing our family. I wouldn't complain one bit about the amount of time we spent working on getting pregnant, only about going along on Malin's daily run.

She couldn't have stopped me though. Most times we ended up on the shore, naked, and in each other's arms before running back to the house.

Malin walked back into the bedroom. "Hey, Dutch?"

"Yes?"

She sat on the edge of the bed that I hadn't gotten out of yet.

"I want you to know that there wasn't anything between me and the guy at DHS."

"It doesn't matter to me if there was or not. You're with me now. But why are you telling me this today?"

"I don't know." She stretched out next to me. "It's been on my mind. It's the only thing that's still left unsaid between us."

I kissed her temple and ran my fingers through her hair. "Ready to run?"

"No. Not anymore."

"Huh?"

"We can run later after it cools down."

"I see. So, what do you want to do instead?"

"I think you know."

Keep reading for a sneak peek
at the next book
in the K19 Security Solutions Series,
**STRIKER!**

# 1

*Striker*

Seeing Aine with another man didn't hurt as bad as I thought it would—it hurt a hell of a lot worse.

She looked happy, though, didn't she? The split second when our eyes met hadn't given me enough time to say for sure.

I watched her walk away with Stuart Anderson, owner of Anderson's Plumbing and all around "nice" guy. Stuart's age had bothered me when I looked him up, but at thirty-one, he was seven years my junior, and instead of being sixteen years older than Aine, Stuart was only nine.

Monk came out the slider and handed me a beer. "Thought you might need one," he said.

"Thanks, man. I must look pretty miserable for you to string five whole words together."

Monk flipped me off and took a swig of his own beer. "The reason I don't laugh at everyone's jokes about how I never talk isn't because I'm shy or whatever the hell you all think about me; it's because they stopped being funny years ago."

"I know. It's just easier to give you shit than it is to face how effed up my own life is."

Monk nodded. "Saylor and I went out for dinner with them a couple of weeks ago."

Saylor was Razor's sister, and I'd heard that she and Monk were spending time together, but I didn't know to what extent. "Aine and Stu?"

"Yeah, but don't call him Stu. He hates it."

"Were you the offending party?"

"Nah, someone else at the brewery said it."

I scrubbed my face with my hand. "I can't believe I'm saying this, Monk, but does she seem happy?"

"He's a plumber."

I turned my head and studied him. "So?"

"You're a former CIA agent who is now a partner in a private intelligence firm. You oughta be able to figure it out." Monk held up his empty bottle. "Want another?"

I nodded. "Thanks, man."

The sun was just about to set on a day I'd been avoiding for eight months. I knew I'd see Aine McNamara again since her sister was married to one of K19's founding partners. I'd just hoped I could finagle my way out of it for several more weeks, or even months. Long enough that I could be certain she'd moved on and was happy. If she hadn't, or wasn't, I might be tempted to tell her that I'd made a horrible mistake when I ended things, and beg her to take me back.

I couldn't do that, though; I was every kind of bad for Aine. She deserved to be with someone who was closer to her own age, someone whom she could build a life with rather than jump into one that was already established. Also, someone who didn't travel ninety percent of the time. The plumber probably never traveled, at least not for work.

There were other reasons we couldn't be together, but I hadn't told her that.

Monk came out to the deck, handed me the beer, and then went back inside, leaving me alone with my thoughts. It was a place where I really didn't want to be, so I went inside too.

"Doc and Merrigan have been delayed. They'll arrive at zero seven hundred tomorrow," said Razor. "You can hang out here and eat or go to the hotel, whichever you'd prefer."

Ranger and Diesel motioned with their heads to leave, and I was happy to join them. It had been a long day, and we were on East Coast time, so it was three hours later for us.

"You can take the SUV," said Monk, handing me the key.

"Can we give you a lift somewhere?" I asked him.

"No, thanks."

Monk was back to his uncommunicative self, but I didn't care. All I wanted to do was go to the hotel and sleep. I just hoped I could, and if I did, I wouldn't dream about Aine.

When I walked into the entrance of the hotel, the first thing I saw was Aine seated at a table with the plumber. A few moments later, two other men joined them at the same time "Stu" gripped the back of her neck with his hand.

I kept watching them, even when Ranger and Diesel walked over to the front desk to check in.

Her profile was illuminated by the table's candlelight, making her look like an angel. As if I'd called out to her, Aine shrugged the plumber's hand away, slowly turned her head, and looked at me. There was no way she could assume I was doing anything other than staring at her.

Our eyes stayed focused on one another's until I saw the plumber about to turn his head. I tore my gaze away and joined Ranger and Diesel at the front desk.

Something about her haunted look before she'd turned toward me ate away at me. What weighed so heavily on her mind? It couldn't be me; she'd obviously moved on with Stu.

Other things that had happened in her life haunted her. Did the plumber know all the trauma she'd been through in the last couple of years? Did he know that her father had lied about his identity her entire life? Did he know that she'd been kidnapped along with two of her closest friends and was held hostage in order to lure out the same man? Did he know she had nightmares nearly every night?

He probably did, and that part was too much for me to think about. The idea that my sweet Aine would lay naked in someone else's arms made every muscle in my body clutch in anger.

# About the Author

I gave myself the gift of writing a book for my birthday one year. A few short years and thirty-plus books later, I've hit a couple of best-seller lists and have had the time of my life. The joy for me is in writing them, but nothing makes me happier than hearing from a reader who tells me I've made her laugh or cry or gasp or hold her breath or stay up all night because she can't put my book down.

The women I write are self-confident, strong, with wills of their own, and hearts as big as the Colorado sky. The men are sublimely sexy, seductive alphas who rise to the challenge of capturing the sweet soul of a woman whose heart they'll hold in the palm of their hand forever. Add in a couple of neck-snapping twists and turns, a page-turning mystery, and a swoon-worthy HEA, and you'll be holding one of my books in your hands.

I love to hear from my readers. You can contact me at heather@heatherslade.com

To keep up with my latest news and releases, please visit my website at www.heatherslade.com to sign up for my newsletter.

# MORE FROM AUTHOR HEATHER SLADE

Made in the USA
Monee, IL
22 October 2021

80599505R10184